Death by Vanity
Be Careful What You Change

Death by Vanity
Be Careful What You Change

Death by Vanity
Be Careful What You Change

Death by Vanity
Be Careful What You Change

Death by Vanity
Be Careful What You Change

Death by Vanity
Be Careful What You Change

Death by Vanity
Be Careful What You Change
By Lena Ma

© Copyright 2020

TABLE OF CONTENTS

Death by Vanity
Be Careful What You Change

Death by Vanity
Be Careful What You Change

THE BEGINNING OF THE END

Our story starts off on a bright and beautiful day in Sunnyvale, California, with the birds chirping and a double rainbow coursing across the blue sky.

We see a trio of women in their early twenties, sitting on the patio in front of a popular and quaint pink flamingo café, a café where customers are free to take pictures with flamingos as well as dress them up for photoshoots, sipping on teacups of organic espresso, and crunching on petite portions of avocado toast adorned with edible flowers.

The sun rays are shining on the lavender silk dress of one of the women, Brielle, radiating her dress into a luminesce of colors as she flips back her long blonde locks over her slim shoulders.

She holds her mini porcelain teacup up to her lips, pinky out, lips bold with crimson red lipstick, and gently giggles as she crosses her right leg over her left, smoothing out the skirt of her dress in the process.

She then takes out her smartphone from her glitter mini crossbody purse, checks the quality of her makeup with her camera, and snaps a portrait of herself running her fingers through her hair, followed by twenty more.

When she finally puts her phone down on the circle glass table in front of her after posting one of those many images on Centriclist, the most popular social sharing app worldwide, the camera switches angles and zooms closer toward her friend, Belle, who is sitting across the table from Brielle, dressed in a royal blue blouse with leather pants and red platform shoes, who also takes her phone out from her purse.

As Belle proceeds to take a picture of herself, she quickly places her phone down and pretends to laugh, as if her friend had just said something funny, when a young man with striking beauty jogs by, one foot in front of the other, flashing a grin at Belle before passing the café.

Belle blushes, flashing back a smile, with her perfectly white teeth glistening from the reflection rays of the sun, and bats her eyes at the man before returning to her camera and proceeding to lift her phone up once more.

She smooths out the curls on her dark brown braids and prepares her facial features for a picture-perfect shot, pursing her lips and pulling in her cheeks. She takes about twenty images of herself before spending the next 10 minutes decorating her best shot with her best filters, posting her picture also on Centriclist with the caption, "Just another boring day."

Briar, one of the more outspoken women in the group, breaks the calm silence, "It's such a beautiful day out today! I've been stuck inside my house all summer, and it's so nice to finally be outside, enjoying the fresh air!"

"Don't you have your own private pool AND movie theater? You can pretty much live in your house all year and still never be bored," Brielle jokingly jabs at Briar for the lavish lifestyle she secretly wishes she also has.

"It's not THAT easy being me! People think I have everything, but look at my Centriclist account! I'm barely reaching 1 million followers! At this rate, I'll never catch up to the grandeur of Kayla Rose. She pretty much flaunts a new ride every day," Briar whines back. "Plus, I don't have a pretty face like yours or Belle's so I can't rely on my looks to boost my popularity!"

"Hey! I have an idea!" Belle interrupts. "There's a trend going on where Centriclisters are taking pictures of themselves while hanging off high cliffs. Let's drive over to Mount Vesuvius and take an epic shot there. That'll definitely boost your following!"

"Hmm...I don't know. That sounds kind of dangerous..." Briar questions.

"No, it's not! I swear! All we need to do is stage it so one of us is holding onto your legs as you dangle off so it looks like you're actually hanging off, but you're not! It's super safe!" Belle continues to claim, excitedly.

"Sounds like a plan to me!" Brielle thrillingly remarks. "Let's go! I'll drive! I know this perfect cliff right off the coast of the Kangie Peak. I go there all the time for my photo ops. It's one of the only places in town where you can actually drive to the summit without having to hike to the top."

"I still think it's stupid, but alright, let's get this over with," Briar sighs as she hops into the front seat of Brielle's hot pink convertible.

As the young women drive toward Mount Vesuvius, they pass hundreds of tourists waiting in line by the Hollywood sign in Los Angeles to take a photograph of themselves with the famous iconic sign.

However, Briar, Brielle, and Belle have been there thousands of times as they live only 15 minutes away and don't see a need to stop for their own breathtaking moments.

As they proceed to drive past the sign, they fail to notice that the people waiting in line are not actually people in the sense that we know.

They are people who have finished taking their pictures with the sign and have frozen in place while attempting to hike down the hill.

Those who have yet to take their turns are too consumed in their own Centriclist feeds to notice their surrounding, fixing their hair and makeup, and choosing the perfect outfits out of many for that perfect picture, distracted by their own egotistical endeavors and vanity to notice the people around them disappearing.

You see, people who take pictures of themselves with the sign, or with any place for that matter, anywhere, never make it out alive. They simply freeze in place as their eyes begin to liquefy, until their bodies eventually turn into glass and shatter into oblivion. This is the cost of the narcissism of human life.

"Road trip!" Belle shouts with her arms up in the air as they near the Kangie Peak at Mount Vesuvius, oblivious to her surroundings as she turns on the radio, surprised to hear her favorite band, The Tasers, playing.

"I love this fucking song! Your vain is shame, ego contagious, step out of the crowd to the best years of your lifeeeee!" She sings, suddenly choking on her words as she hears a mysterious sound. "What was that? Did you guys hear that?"

"Hear what?" Brielle asks. "I didn't hear anything."

"It sounded like...like someone was crying, like someone was in pain."

"Oh, Belle, I'm sure you're just imagining things again. You always let your imagination get the best of you," Brielle assures.

"Girls! I think this calls for a road trip selfie! Say 'cheese'!" Briar announces as she pulls out her phone and signals Brielle and Belle to squeeze their faces toward hers. "Let's make this the PERFECT day to remember!"

"Ooooo, make sure to get the beach in the background. #beachlife bitches!" Belle exclaims as she holds out a peace sign and sticks her tongue out at the camera.

"On the count of three, we all strike the best pose. Ready? One, two, three!" Briar calls out, her right arm extended out in front of her, as she snaps a picture of her with her friends.

"Okay, now let's see, what filter to use...Brielle!! WATCH OUT!!!!"

Briar points toward the road where a young teenage girl is standing still as Brielle loses control of her car from the distraction of the photograph.

Belle slams her fist repeatedly against Brielle's horn and yells at the girl to move out of the way; however, the girl does not seem to hear her.

Briar, too, notices that Brielle is losing control of the steering wheel and lunges forward to take it from her.

"Brielle!! What the fuck is wrong with you!? Didn't you see that...that...uhhh...Brielle?!??" Briar asks, frightened, as she turns toward Brielle and notices black slime spilling out of her eye sockets, dripping down her cheeks, as if she is in a horror movie.

"HOLY FUCKING SHIT!! WHAT THEY FUCK, BRIELLE!?!?" Briar screams as she scurries away from Brielle, the steering wheel losing control as the convertible collides into a barren oak tree off the side of the road.

Crash.

"Brielle? Belle? Is anyone there?" Briar weakly asks moments after the collision as she pushes a crumbled car door off her mangled body, blood aggressively dripping down her face, arms, and legs from non-fatal injuries.

"Hello?"

Struggling to stand up, she limps over to the other side of the car as Belle pushes another door off her.

"Belle? Are you okay?" Briar asks as she limps toward Belle, relieved that she is not the only one left alive.

"Yeah, I'm okay, I think. Where's Brielle?" Belle asks, disoriented, a shard of glass from the window jabbing into the left side of her abdomen.

"I...I...don't know. One minute she looked like she was possessed, and the next, we're making out with a tree. Brielle!! Brielle!!" Briar calls out, seeing nothing except for piles of fine glass shards which she assumes is from the shattered windows of the wrecked car.

"Bri..."

Briar stops in her tracks as she finds her foot inches deep inside a puddle of black tar, confused as to where it came from as she has never seen or felt anything like it before, a substance both thick and smooth, both warm and chilling.

"Hey, Belle! Come look at this! I found something really weird," Briar calls out with no answer in return.

"Belle?"

Still no response, and now slightly irritated from feeling ignored, Briar looks around and finds Belle standing still off to the side of the barren road, gazing out into the distance of the ocean beside them, blood dripping from the tips of her fingers with her back turned toward Briar.

Briar stomps over to where Belle's back faces her, unnaturally stiff, and puts a hand on her shoulder.

"Belle, didn't you hear me calling?"

As Briar turns Belle's body around, she is faced with darkness, a black hole of bleakness stemming from deep inside her eyes, as if her sockets had been hollowed out and replaced with nothingness.

Suddenly, a strange black and thick liquid, similar to the substance Briar had seen dripping from Brielle's eyes, begins to trickle out of Belle's sockets, covering the surfaces of her face and body, until it finally consumes her as her stiff pale body spontaneously shatters, the fine shards floating away with the brisk wind.

"What the fuck is happening!?" Briar backs away in fear as she had just witnessed her best friend fragment into thin air, a sight she struggles to believe as reality.

"No, no! This can't be real! This can't be real!"

Still in disbelief, Briar runs away from the scene of horror, praying that it was all a dream and that her friends are both still very alive. She continues running until she sees the beautiful waves of the beach with seemingly normal people around her.

They're okay. Thank God. These people are okay. It must have just been a dream. In fact, I'll send a picture to Bri and Belle right now, and I guarantee, they will respond within seconds! Briar thinks to herself, reassuring her mind that the car accident was all a terrible nightmare, and her friends are still okay.

She prances over to the turquoise waters, runs her fingers through her long beach locks, and snaps a photo of herself with the sunset overlooking in the background.

As she prepares to send her picture to Brielle and Belle, she notices small drops of black liquid dripping onto the glass of her phone.

"Someone better not be dripping their charcoal ice cream on me, or I'm going to freak!" Briar announces as she looks up and, to her surprise, sees no one near her.

What? Whatever. Briar ignores the blackness and continues with her message.

"What a perfect way to end a beautiful day! #blessed." Just as she hits "send," her face begins to feel wet, and as she runs her fingers over her cheeks, she is met with a black tar-like substance on the tips of her fingers.

Before she can summon the voice to react to the situation, her fate is met with stiffness to her body and soul, cracks forming along the skin of her being, until she finally breaks like a porcelain doll and shatters, her remains sprinkling into the desert sand, washed away by the waves as her phone remains on the shore with over eighty notifications of likes and comments from her Centriclist followers.

THE PANDEMIC ASCENDS

A harsh thunderstorm blares in the distance. Rain pours down from the dark sky onto the pueblo-style clay homes in the middle of the deserted city of Armazo.

The population in the town of Armazo is a measly 50 people, but everyone remains antisocial and keeps to themselves.

It is a dark Sunday afternoon as two friends, Amber and Jessica, scurry under the shelter of an umbrella perked up on a lonely table beside the only café in town.

"The rain's really coming down, isn't it? I should have brought an umbrella," Amber shivers to Jessica, her arms crossed over the front of her body as she attempts to dry herself off with the bottom of her long bohemian paisley skirt.

"I know! Me too! Where the hell did this rain even come from? It never rains here. Like, never! I was beginning to think we're living in a drought. I don't even own an umbrella!" Jessica remarks, squeezing and twisting puddles of water out from her blonde highlighted locks.

"Oooo! I need a picture for my Centriclist; otherwise, no one would ever believe that it's raining in one of the driest towns in the world. #rainqueen!" She proclaims as she snaps a picture of herself smiling while pointing to her clothes and hair drenched from the rain of the storm.

"Maybe we can make a run for it. My aunt lives about two blocks from here. If we book it, we can probably get there scar-free and camp out until the rain stops. I haven't spoken to her in years after the fallout she had with my mom, but I'm sure she'll at least let us in to dry off. What do you think, Jess?" Amber shouts over the sound of the strong winds, proud of her quick-witted idea as she checks to make sure her white platform sandals didn't track too much sand while running through the desert.

However, Jessica does not answer. She remains silent, staring off into the distance, the side of her right cheek facing Amber.

"Jess? Are we making a run for it or what? I'm getting drenched! Jess?" Amber reaches over to touch Jessica's shoulder in an attempt to grab her attention.

As Jessica turns toward her, Amber sees a thick midnight black liquid oozing from the corners of Jessica's eyes, trickling down her chin, and onto her white laced blouse, turning her pristine new top into the darkness of the sky as the rain continues to pour from the vehement clouds.

Amber screams in terror as her friend suddenly begins to secrete an unknown black substance from all parts of her body, coming out through her ears and nose, as well as continuing to ooze from her eyes.

"Jess!?" Amber cries in horror and disbelief.

She rubs her own eyes with her fingers as she cannot believe what she is seeing. More and more of this strange black substance continues to engulf Jessica's once well-kempt body until it finally starts to crack like a porcelain doll, shattering into small glass shards of smithereens, and blowing away with the gust of wind.

Still confused and terrified, Amber glances around her surroundings. One by one, she sees the once locals also beginning to disappear. The town's only bus driver, always eager to greet his passengers, begins to leak this strange black substance from the corners of his eyes as the liquid soon consumes him, causing him to shatter as the passengers on the bus lose their minds and scream in fear of death, the vehicle making a wrong turn and crashing into the side of the desert mountain, combusting as flaming passengers roll onto the asphalt ground.

Amber then looks over to her right and sees a little boy, no more than 8-years old, standing in the middle of the road, while a car heads toward him.

"Hey! Hey! Little boy! Move out of the way!" Amber screams as she runs toward the boy to get him out of the way of the moving vehicle.

However, when she places her right hand on his shoulder, the little boy turns around, eyes dripping with the same black substance as everyone else, before also shattering into glass smithereens himself, his phone dropping onto the black asphalt.

What is going on? Amber wonders as she gawks at the people around her. Many of them, people she had seen in her area but have never spoken to, are trudging through the roads in lazy, erratic patterns, almost as if they are zombies who have give up on life.

One minute, they are normal and upbeat individuals going about their days and posting on social media, and the next, within the blink of an eye, they transform into zombie-like form, with no knowledge or recollection of their surroundings or what is happening to them.

Death by Vanity
Be Careful What You Change

Amber's heart begins to beat faster as she sees a familiar man standing below a street lamp. Amber knows who this man is. She recognizes how his dark black bangs are always parted off to the left side of his face, his bangs longer than the rest of his head of hair.

She went on a blind date with him last week after she had asked Jessica to set her up with one of her friends, as she was tired of being single since her ex-boyfriend of seven years left her for a younger woman fresh out of college.

Not wanting to confront him, as she has been ghosting him for days because she finds him incredibly arrogant and dull, Amber turns the other way, just when she hears a loud thud, followed by a high-pitched scream.

"Somebody help him!" She overhears a woman shriek, backing up into the small crowd behind her before bolting away, leaving the seizing body behind for others to deal with, as Amber turns back to the sound of the cry.

While the woman screams, she can hear the blood in her own body rushing to her ears before she fumbles with her car key and swings around the corner of the café to her Porsche.

Amber races toward the crowd and sees her blind date trembling and twisting on the ground, also covered in this midnight substance. Strangely, no one is moving to help him; they remain quiet and still, either in shock or in oblivion.

Seconds later, he, too, shatters into dark ash shards as those around him slowly stiffen in silence, their eyes also seeping with this black liquid as they continue standing, untouched. The street becomes quiet.

What the hell is happening here? First, Jess, and now, it looks like the whole town is fucked up. Amber fearfully contemplates to herself, afraid that there's something bigger beyond her lurking close in the distance.

She rummages through her purse for her phone, hoping she can catch her mother in time before she leaves for her job at the library. Amber has no idea what's going on, but she sure as hell doesn't want anyone else, especially someone close to her, to find out first-hand.

Maybe there's something in the air, but whatever or whoever it is, the outdoors seems to be the worst place to be right now.

"Come on, come on. Pick up. Pick up!" Amber anxiously speaks into her phone as she continues to hear the deafening sound of ringing on the other end.

No luck. Desperate, she tries several more times when, suddenly, a car swerves from around the corner of the café.

The woman Amber had seen earlier begins maniacally speeding down the dirt road, turning the shattered shards into a raging dust storm, until she finally stops in the middle of a sand dune. She stumbles out of her car, places a glistening tiara on her head, and begins to shout into her phone as she streams live on Centriclist.

"My name is Delilah Hamilton! Delilah Hamilton! I do not deserve to be ignored anymore. I deserve to be heard. I shall not be ignored! I shall not be forgotten!" Delilah screams for several seconds, right arm out in front of her and left arm up in the air, until she suddenly freezes up.

Amber watches Delilah as her entire body remains still except for the strange black substance streaming out from beneath her eyelids.

Seconds later, her body starts trembling at an unimaginable speed before splintering into a million tiny fragments, almost as if the most delicate porcelain doll has fallen off a cliff and onto the ruins of an old car, her phone spilling out of her hand and into the crevices of the dusty sand.

Amber covers her mouth with her forearm to fade out the shrilling shriek she has pent up inside her as the woman combusts. Thousands of little glass pieces soon coat the desert sand, small, flesh-toned flakes drift in the cold air where a body once was.

I must be hallucinating. This must be a dream. Amber thinks as she pinches the palm of her left hand.

Hallucination. That's the only possible answer to all this. This is insane. I must be crazy. There's no way this can be real. It's like I'm in a fucking movie!

"Come on, mom! Pick up! Pick up the fucking phone!" Amber continues to call her mother, with no luck in sight.

Suddenly, she jumps as another car comes swerving toward her, the wheels spinning against the thick and heavy fine shards of people scattered along the road.

The tail end of the car swings out, the vehicle reeling in circles as Amber watches in horror while it collides into a barren tree and combusts into flames. Thin tendrils of smoke drift up from beneath the crumpled hood while the driver's door hangs open in disarray.

The man inside dangles halfway out, his face covered in crimson blood caused by a large laceration sliced across his forehead.

"Sir! Sir! Are you alright?" Amber rushes over to the man, attempting to twist and pull the seat belt off him, but the belt remains locked tight as the clip has been crushed.

Damn it! Where's my pocket knife when I need it? The one day I forget to carry it with me is the one and only day I need it.

The smoke beneath the hood of the automobile begins to rise, the flames turning into a glowing blaze. As the thick embers continue to surge higher and higher, the top of the car compresses further into the man.

"Almost there. We're almost there. I'm going to get you out, sir. Just a little bit further," Amber chants on as she continues wrestling with the belt and pulling out the man while he yelps in agony.

However, the screams of the crying man shortly turn into silent tremors as Amber notices black stains on her light blue leather jacket.

What the fuck? Amber thinks, attempting to wipe away the stains as she looks up and sees the black substance trickling out from the corners of the man's eyes, engulfing him until he, too, finally shatters, his remains fueling the fire of the car as Amber steps back in disbelief, watching the vehicle spontaneously explode into debris.

Her heart pounds vigorously against her chest, threatening to escape her rib cage. Her hand trembles as she lifts it up to her own face to wipe off the sludge that the remains of the man had splattered onto her. The dark substance coats her fingers like cement, a substance unlike any she has ever seen before.

All she can do is scream.

I just want to go home. I just want to go home. Please make this stop. Make this stop! Amber cries to herself, closing her eyes to deflect from reality, wishing she's in bed right now instead of in the midst of this chaos.

Then, she hears something, a faint cry from a distance that resembles the wind in agony.

What the fuck is that? Amber looks around her surroundings but sees nothing.

She turns back around and tries to scope out the best method to make it to her aunt's house in the midst of the pouring thunderstorm without turning into the black substance and glass ash herself.

She hears the noise again. This time, from a closer distance. Still, nothing in sight. But the noise continues to creep closer and closer behind her. Panicking, Amber looks around frantically, from her left to her right.

Nothing. She looks again. Left to right. Nothing.

As the storm begins to die down, Amber suspects it's safe enough to make a run for it. She needs to get indoors or else she would surely be killed with the rest of these poor souls out here.

"Just one more picture to remember this moment. I live in such a boring town that something freaky like this will probably only happen once every thousand years!" Amber speaks to herself as she takes a self-portrait, pretending to be in shock in front of the crushed vehicle.

Glancing around to make sure cars are not heading her way, Amber steps off the curb, gets into her running stance, and freezes. The small town around her continues to combust in disarray as Amber remains frozen in her place.

Moments later, Amber's eyes begin liquefying with the same evolving black substance as a silver glow encompasses her, and her body shatters into a million pieces.

OBLIVION OF IGNORANCE

"Welcome to the first ever EXCLUSIVE Centriclist influencer party, where only the most famous and popular prevail. Let us all raise a toast to us, the top influencers of the decade, with many, many more years to come! Cheers!"

"CHEERS!"

As Clare watches her guests celebrate with champagne and cocktails in her rented luxury mansion, she can't help but reflect back on several years ago, when she was just another ordinary person, with no interest or presence in social media.

Clare used to travel the world, a culturalist who was truly interested in getting to know and live like locals in the countries she visited. She spent months at a time in various countries, adopting the customs, learning the language, and getting to know those who live outside of popular tourist areas.

However, one day, while working on a coffee plantation in Colombia, Clare heard about the release of a new cutting-edge social media app known as "Centriclist," an app that allows users to instantly rise to fame and fortune by posting their best selves online.

Desperate for money, and tired of working multiple jobs in every country she visited to support her nomadic lifestyle, Clare decided to create an account as a traveler, posting images of herself visiting the many countries she wanders even though she had never taken a single picture of her world travels before.

Less than six months later, her presence on Centriclist skyrocketed to popularity and fortune, with over 10 million followers and making $5,000 per post. She was hooked.

Clare could not believe how much attention she was getting and how much money she was making by just posting a few images of herself in front of iconic world destinations. She loves how she is instantly recognized by all wherever she goes.

However, because she had let all that fame go inside her head, Clare has forgotten all the reasons she began traveling in the first place, turning her once culture-focused lifestyle into visiting only the hot tourist destinations in every country, focusing more on taking the best images of herself to showcase to her fans and neglecting the humble lives of locals as she destroys and exposes their towns for pictures rather than interacting with them.

Her most memorable incident is when she was thrown into a prison in Moscow, Russia for defacing the country flag by cutting a hole in the middle and posting an image of herself wearing a bikini. Her behavior blew up the news worldwide, and although it got her in trouble with the Russian government, it was that same image that helped

Clare gain millions more followers, an event she does not regret despite spending over a year locked up.

Fuck them anyway. They don't know good publicity even if it slapped them in their stupid faces.

"Hey, Clare, you ready for a refill or what?" Jonah interrupts her thoughts, bringing Clare back into the present moment, as he walks over to her with his signature grin and twinkling blue eyes, holding a pitcher of a mysterious mixed beverage.

Clare shakes her head and weakly smiles back, "No thanks, Jonah, I need to pace myself when it comes to your insane concoctions, or I'll throw up over the couch again. Hey, do you mind stepping back a few steps? I look so fucking hot right now, and I need to take this picture of my maybe stolen dress before you or someone else spills rum all over it," Clare takes a few steps back, positioning herself in front of the beautiful marble fireplace, and takes five images of herself, each one with a different posture and facial expression.

"You tell him, babe," Clare's Centriclist boyfriend, Hunter, comes up to them and gives Clare a long and passionate kiss on her lips, wrapping his arms around her and squeezing her close to him. "It feels so good to finally touch you in person, you hot piece of sexiness. You know, Jonah, it technically doesn't count as getting laid when your victims are passed out."

"Oh, whatever, you guys are no fun. I'm just trying to spice up this lame excuse for a party. Later, dudes," Jonah responds as he throws out a peace sign and skips away.

Clare remains silent. Despite her long list of reckless behaviors, stealing included, alcohol never really does it for her.

However, because she is in a room surrounded by powerful influencers who can make or break her with the click of a button, she can't risk doing or saying anything that would have her labeled as "social outcast."

"Take a photo together as our official coming out as a couple announcement?" Hunter asks cheerfully, pulling out his phone.

"Sure," Clare responds with a soft smile, "Anything for my boyfriend."

Clare never had a boyfriend before in her life. She never thought she would ever settle down for anyone, choosing a life of drifting and promiscuity over stability.

Now that she has one, she wants to see how it goes and avoid doing anything to jeopardize it.

"Say #cybercouple!" Hunter shouts as he snaps a picture of himself kissing Clare on the cheek.

"Cyber couple? That's quite an announcement. I think this calls for some Dom Pérignon. Clare gets the first glass, of course. We all know she desperately needs one," Bill saunters up and drapes his bony arm around Clare's shoulders.

"She's been a stick in the mud since I first slipped into her DMs; it's time to see if she has any feelings other than anger and sarcasm."

Clare jerks away from him and rolls her eyes while the others chuckle. She has no comeback for Bill; he was right. She isn't necessarily a mean person; she just has a difficult time caring about people she doesn't care about.

Especially stupid people. Like Bill. He isn't a bad person per se, she just...wouldn't mind if he suddenly vanishes from the face of the planet.

"Aww, come on, Bill, leave her alone. She had a rough night. Losing 100,000 followers in one day can put anyone in a terrible mood."

Hunter senses the discomfort and pulls Clare to his side. "Why don't you take this champagne and see if the twins need a refill over there?"

He nods to the corner by the grand piano, where a group of people are huddled around Jonah, waiting for that sweet pour. In the center of that group are two identical twins, identical down to the way they smile, speak, and walk.

The first twin is Todd, a handsome and brooding man, by most standards, with typical model-like features like blonde hair and blue eyes. Beside him is his sister, Kayla, also with blonde hair and blue eyes, and recently voted one of the most beautiful women in the world.

They have always been the most relaxed among the Centriclist influencers, exuding a natural cool and chill vibe that many have strived to accomplish.

Todd and Kayla are known as the powerhouses on Centriclist. They are both self-proclaimed models who always seem to have images of themselves taken in front of extravagant places, such as off the side of mountains, on top of planes, and inside cages of vicious tigers.

Clare never knows how they are able to reach such extravagant lengths and still maintain perfect physiques. Post after post, they always manage to get over a million likes, a feat Clare always questions is real.

"OMG, guys! Madilyn Models just messaged me, and they want to sign me on as one of their runway GODDESSES!!!" Kayla squeals as the amped up and drunk crowd cheers along with her.

"#goddess!" Kayla takes a photo of herself with her fingers combing through her hair and lips pursed together before posting her news on her Centriclist feed.

Hunter leans over and gives Clare a passionate kiss on the lips as Bill marches away in hopes of striking up better conversation.

"Don't worry, everyone loves Kayla, but you'll always be my number one," Hunter whispers softly into Clare's right ear.

Clare smiles at him and opens her mouth to begin to speak.

"Ladies and Gentlemen! Influencers from all over! Thank you for coming to my Centriclist party. As you all know, and the reason you're all here, Centriclist has become a big part of our social lives. Hell, it's how we all met! It's the reason we all stand here today as the best of the best. I don't know about you guys, but I, for one, cannot live without the idea of knowing that I can take a picture of myself whenever I look fantastic and posting it online. It's so satisfying! Kayla, we all know you've been the queen of selfies for years now, so we all expect you to bring it big time!

Throughout this party, I want you all to post your images on your feeds. Whoever obtains the most likes by the end of this party gets a very 'special' surprise!" Clare finishes as she gives Bill a wink.

The door suddenly swings open as a strong gust of wind blows over the candelabra sitting on the table by the front door.

"Oh my GOD, you guys! It's CRAZY outside. It took me like 30 minutes to get here! Did you all start without me? Of course, you did, the whole town did from the looks of it."

The last member of the influencers comes breezing into the room – Brooke. She is, and has always been, the life of the party, the sweet girl-next-door willing to drop anything and everything for the sake of a good time.

Brooke throws her coat onto the green velvet couch and slicks her hair back into a ponytail.

"Alright, Jonah. I've been dreaming all day about what kind of vile mixture you would come up with tonight, and now, I'm here and ready. Hit me!"

Jonah laughs as he gives her a quick hug, "You got it, girl. What do you mean the whole town got started without you? It's still early; Mikey's doesn't close for another four hours."

Brooke nods emphatically, "Oh, don't I know it! But you would think they'd shut it down early. I passed, like, four people just stumbling around, absolutely hammered. One guy even fell flat on his face, practically in front of my car, stiff as a board!"

She pauses to accept a full glass of tequila sunrise from Jonah. "Thanks. Anyway, there must be something besides rain in the air. People are acting crazy, almost like they are possessed."

"Well, as long as you're here now! Group huddle for the best selfies of our lives. We need something to remember our first night together in person! Smile!"

The group huddles together as Jonah takes a slightly crooked picture of the group, Brooke bending over to tie her shoe and missing the shot.

Clare could have sworn that, at that very moment that Jonah took the shot, she heard the faintest echo of a voice crying out, begging for mercy. It lasted only for a moment before the voice suddenly stopped.

However, no one else seemed to hear it, so Clare shrugs it off and asks the twins to crank the music up. She will have a good time tonight, come hell or high water.

THE INFLUENCERS THREATENED

"What the hell was that?" Bill jerks up from his phone and asks.

A passive, high-pitched scream fills the air, interrupting the music and fun. Clare sits up from lying on the couch and peers through the window, her eyes straining against the darkness to see what's going on as the night befalls upon them. The road looks empty, with shadows lurking in the dark, a seemingly quiet night other than the strange cries.

There's that sound again. Who is out there howling like a banshee at this hour? Clare presses her hand to the window above her eyes, eliminating the glare that the strobe light is causing.

The music cuts out as more of the influencers rush over to peek out the window.

"What's going on out there?"

"I don't know."

"Can you see anything?"

"No, what about you?"

Suddenly, a strange woman, covered in what looks like black paint, collides into the window of the old mansion, startling Clare as her heart begins to beat faster and faster.

Behind the woman, she can hear car alarms blaring as both vehicles and people crash into each other, resulting in some sort of freak zombie accident.

"Help me! For the love of God, HELP ME! Don't let it get me! Don't let it get me! Let me in! LET ME IN!" The woman cries as she presses the palm of her bloody hands against the glass.

Turning around toward the crowd, Clare shouts, "We need to let her in! She'll die out there!"

Brooke interjects, "No, DON'T! I've heard about this. I thought it was just a rumor. I didn't actually think it would come true. I should have known better! Everyone out there is already infected. There's nothing we can do to help. The best thing we can do is stay inside and save ourselves. Any contact with that air can be deadly."

"Why? What's out there? What air?" Clare asks curiously, demanding answers.

"I don't know, but whatever it is, it's causing people to bleed some sort of black substance from their eye sockets and then spontaneously shatter into a million pieces.

However, it has been rumored that right before this happens, a cry is heard from a close distance, a cry that resembles howling wind in agony, and that anyone who comes into contact with this infected air after hearing this cry will immediately shatter.

I don't know exactly what's going on out there, but I damn well don't want to find out. I think that as long as we stay indoors, we should be fine. True, we heard the cry, but as long as we don't come into contact with the air, we should be safe," Brooke tries to reassure the crowd.

"What the FUCK is going on!? Get me out of here! Get me out of here!" Kayla begins to freak. "I'm too young to die!"

The screaming woman outside cries louder. The guests inside begin whispering. Two of the influencers huddle inside a small, cramped closet, biting their cuticles and pulling their hair out in anxiety.

Clare turns toward the window again, confused, and watches as several local bystanders rush over to the window to pull the screaming woman away from the mansion. Halfway across the front lawn, they all stop dead in their tracks and remain eerily still, not a single movement in sight.

Clare sucks in her breath.

Bill gags.

Kayla screams somewhere from behind.

Brooke shrieks and buries her face into Hunter's chest, who wraps his shaking arms around her and can only look on with wide eyes and a slack jaw.

The black substance. Copious amounts of thick, midnight liquid ooze down their pale faces. Their eyes become unrecognizable, as if they had turned to melted flesh. They scream in anguish and clutch at their eyes, writhing, trying desperately to prevent their bodies from liquefying.

The substance pours thicker as their skin begins to crack like porcelain dolls. The ooze fills the cracks of their skin, taking away from them their resemblance of human beings. All at once, they collapse onto the ground, their bodies twisting and contorting as if some sort of puppet string holding them upright had snapped.

Neighbors soon begin to emerge from their homes across the street, racing outside to see what the commotion is all about. Probably hopeful for the chance of snagging an epic shot for their Centriclist profiles. The influencers still inside the house anxiously begins to shout and pound their fists against the windows from inside the mansion, hysterically trying to warn them.

Stop! Run the other way! Go back!

But they are too late. The confusion on the neighbors' faces turn into shock as they soon also shatter to oblivion.

Their eyes virtually dissolve, replaced by streams of the vile black substance that begins running from their cheeks down to their chins, streaming down their necks toward their chests, soaking their clothes and filling their mouths.

Clare stares as, one by one, they too fall onto the ground. She watches the way their bodies thrash and their blood pools, the remains of their bodies floating away with the passing wind.

One of the victims crawls and scrapes his way across the lawn in an attempt to beg for help. Instead, he is faced with his own fate.

The remaining bodies on the front lawn splinter, raining down flesh-toned, glass-like pieces that blend in with the faint patches of grass growing from the dirt ground. Kayla screams again, refusing to stop until her voice gives out on her.

A chilling sensation runs down Clare's spine as the bodies sprinkle before her very eyes, forming the words, "You're next."

"You're next?! What the hell does that mean!?" Bill shouts.

"I DON'T WANT TO DIE!!" Jonah screams as he runs around the living room, pushing over chairs and knocking down the glass trinkets placed neatly on the mantle of the fireplace.

"What the FUCK is going on!?" Kayla panics as she runs to her purse, digging for her phone while Clare and the others continue to watch the madness unfold outside.

More people dropping to the ground, more black substance turning the peaceful desert into midnight magma.

"Hello? I-I need to report an emergency, there's...there's people literally dropping d-dead outside. I think they're dying. They're bleeding some sort of black liquid everywhere and having seizures and— NO, I'M NOT CRAZY!! I KNOW WHAT I'M SEEING! YOU'RE CRAZY! Don't you dare hang up on me! Don't hang up on me!! We need help! WE NEED HELP!!" Kayla screams into her phone as the cops on the other end refuse to believe her.

Realizing the cops aren't going to be much help, Clare turns her attention to the door, watching as the infamously moronic Bill pulls on his coat and boots. That clearly isn't a smart idea, considering everyone who stepped foot outside seemed to die...

Clare looks at Bill, "You're not going to make it if you go out there," she says, her voice emotionless. "You should stay here."

Bill shakes his head vehemently, looking queasy.

"I need to go home and check on my mom. She's all alone tonight and was recently discharged from the hospital for depression. I can't risk having anything trigger her while I'm not there. I need to go," he forces a laugh and tries to lighten his tone. "Besides, the last thing I need is her wandering around the streets in her nightgown looking for me."

With his hand placed gently on the doorknob, Bill takes a deep breath and leaves, the wooden door slamming behind him as the others begin to murmur and gather close around the window to watch his fate.

Not long after stepping off the front porch, the same deadly black substance begins to leak from Bill's blue eyes, first in thin rivulets, then in large pools.

Bill stumbles for a moment, attempting to shake off the uneasy feeling he is experiencing, but then continues to stride forward as best he can.

The rest of the guests can see him visibly gritting his teeth, trying to fight whatever is trying to overtake his body. Bill tries to push past the pain and the substance that continues to consume him, continuing to push forward to get home to his mother.

Unfortunately, like all the others, he soon falls victim to the deadly air, his body crashing onto the ground as he enters an uncontrollable seizure.

Clare sighs and traces the name of the forgotten Bill in the fog that formed on the glass.

Darwinism at its finest, she thinks. *I told him so.*

Kayla breaks into tears as Bill continues to contort on the drenched dirt, cracks appearing along his cheeks and forehead, spreading up and down, left and right, until they finally cover every inch of his visible skin.

One, two, three, Clare counts as she watches the convulsions.

Sure enough, on 'three' the fitness influencer shatters into a million tiny pieces.

AWAKENING & BETRAYAL

"This night is a somber one for not only our town, but our country also, as we sit and wait, terrified, for the official statement regarding the unforeseen, and rather unprecedented, pandemic," a reporter announces through Hunter's laptop.

Clare leans forward from her perch on the window, eyes glued to the screen. The others had collapsed into a haphazard pile on the floor, holding each other and sniffling as they strain to listen to the reporter's words.

"Although we don't have much information yet, the reports we do have is gravely alarming. Across the nation, people are leaving their homes, only to be struck down within minutes by a mysterious illness.

Symptoms of this yet unnamed disease include bleeding a strange black substance from the eyes and violent convulsions caused by seizures. Shortly after these seizures begin, the infected person will appear to crack, with deep lines running across his or her skin.

Only minutes later, that infected person will experience what is effectively being called 'shattering', fragmenting into glass shards and disintegrating into thin air. At this time, we strongly encourage everyone to stay inside, and stay safe.

For your sake and everyone else's, do not leave your homes! From Channel 6, this is Isabella Robinson, now signing off."

The broadcast suddenly turns off the air, a pitch-black screen appearing on Hunter's laptop in place of the live program. Clare settles back into her spot and looks outside once more.

Of all the things she had seen outside that evening, only the burning cars remain. But even those are dying too. She picks at a fleck of dirt beneath her fingernail as her guests begin to argue.

"We should all stay here," Todd declares as he looks nervously out the window.

The rain is pouring down heavier now, combined with strong winds blowing both cars and people through the air.

Kayla shakes her head and clutches her phone while tears streak down her face. "No, I want to go. I need to go home! My hungry puppy is home all alone, and I think I left the stove on. I need to go!"

"Todd's right, though. We should all stay together and not go outside for any reason. It's pretty much life or death here," Brooke insists.

"It's better just to face it," Jonah speaks in Kayla's defense. "Why bother delaying the inevitable? It's a freaking virus, for Christ's sake! It's not like any of us are going to make it anyway. It's either die now, or die later."

Brooke shoots a cynical look toward Jonah, "Are you serious? You just want to roll over and let it take you?"

"Well, it's easy for you to say, Brooke! Don't you think it's rather convenient of you to show up JUST when shit's hitting the fan?" Hunter points his finger.

"WHAT?! Are you accusing ME of this?! Are you insane?!" Brooke shouts back.

"I'm just saying, it seems rather suspicious that everything fucked up just as you show up LATE to the party. Where exactly were you anyway!?" Hunter continues to accuse Brooke.

"I don't have time for your bullshit, Hunt. I've already explained myself. There's no point in trying to explain myself to people who won't listen."

The live broadcast suddenly flickers to life again, interrupting their argument. The woman from before reappears on screen, her face drawn, and the whites of her eyes appear to be red and swollen.

"Hello, and good evening. If any of you missed our earlier broadcast from just a few moments ago, we would like to recap: there is a deadly virus spreading rapidly throughout the counties. Symptoms include a dark substance material bleeding from the eyes and violent seizures shortly before death.

The illness sets in quickly and without any warning. Initially, we believed it to be a domestic virus, contained only to our country, but as more reports flood in, we have reason to believe that this deadly virus is spreading rapidly across the globe."

Isabella pauses to sniffle and raise a tissue to her face. She dabs at her eyes before focusing on the camera once more. There is audible crying in the background as the camera trembles.

Clare cannot take her eyes away from the screen. This is real, whatever it is. Not only is it destroying their little town – it is annihilating the entire world.

Suddenly, Clare hears a noise to her left and turns to see Todd and Kayla leave the room to grab their coats.

Those idiots are really going to try to make it home.

"Come on, Todd. Let's go. I need to go!" Kayla pleads as she tugs on Todd's sleeve.

"No, wait. I think I'd rather stay. I don't want to risk my life by going out there, and neither should you." Todd resists, slowing laying his coat on the chair beside him.

"This is ridiculous! There's nothing out there! All we need to do is stick in some earplugs, and we'll be fine. We can't turn unless we hear that god-awful noise. Now, let's go!" Kayla persists.

"Fine, fine! But one more picture to remember this day by. This is such a once-in-a-lifetime occurrence, and I definitely need to post this to keep up with the crowd. Jonah, scoot over to your left so I can get a good shot of that black sludge," Todd compromises as he takes his phone out before the two of them head out the front door.

Clare shakes her head in disappointment. She expected this from Kayla, but Todd is usually the more reasonable one. There is no way they will survive. She turns back toward the screen as the reporter clears her throat once more.

"As of this moment, the virus is believed to be airborne in nature, entering through the corneas of its victims' eyes, taking hold of their optic nerves, and working its way toward the frontal lobe of the brain. Neurologists have speculated that, eventually, the virus will reach the cerebellum, the part of the brain responsible for voluntary movements.

Once the cerebellum has been confiscated by this mysterious, yet dangerous, virus, the nerves will short-circuit, causing the human body to seize. Because of its novelty, scientists have not yet discovered the cause behind this 'shattering' effect.

At this current point in time, public health experts are urging citizens to stay in their homes and limit contact with the air as much as possible, as even a single breath of the toxic air can prove fatal. Thank you for tuning in this evening. We will alert the general public as we hear more. Stay home, and stay safe."

Clare, Jonah, Brooke, and Hunter quickly turn their heads around as the front door slams. They rush to the window and watch as Todd hastily backs his Ferrari out of the driveway and into the dusty road.

However, the car barely makes it to the corner of the street before it collides with a barren tree and careens out of control.

Inside the car, the remaining influencers can see the side of Todd's skeletal face press up against the window, streams of the midnight black substance flowing down his anguished face. Beside him, lies Kayla, seizing and contorting in the passenger seat, the substance running down the side of her cheeks, dripping onto her $5,000 haute couture dress.

The car continues to spin out of control as Todd and Kayla both slowly disintegrate into the cold, thin air, eventually crashing into one of the many wrecked vehicles that surround it and combusts into flames.

Shocked and terrified, the group tears themselves away from the Victorian window and panics, half of whom are praying to some external force who can save them from this city of destruction while the rest sees this chaos as an opportunity for attention and fame. Hunter curses and leans his head against the wall…Clare looks on with a stoic indifference.

"Well…what the fuck do we do now?" Hunter asks, his question directed toward Jonah, who paces back and forth by the substance-stained window, wiping his tears with the back of his hand in an attempt to preserve his manhood. "We can't go out there; just look at what's happening to people who do! We're quickly running out of food, and from the looks of it, absolutely nobody is going to come and rescue us."

Outside the mansion, people are continuing to exit their homes out of desperation or disbelief that the virus actually exists, running into the empty streets like children on a playground. Nevertheless, none of them make it very far as the virus instantly overtakes their beings, leading them to their fates.

Clare watches in dubious fascination as more and more people drop to the ground. What had once been a peaceful, quiet desert terrain now looks like a scene from a war movie. Some of the bodies shatter immediately upon hitting the ground. Others prolong, convulsing violently, then twitching more delicately, before finally succumbing to the virus' strength.

Yet, Clare finds it intriguing how some people seem to be able to fight back against it while others seem to instead perish at the first symptom.

Hunter sighs loudly and shakes his head, "Maybe we can go outside if we find some gas masks or something. Those should probably keep the virus away."

Brooke looks out the window. Some people had already fashioned face masks out of scarves, thinking that those would protect them from the mysterious element. Others are wearing gas masks, just as Hunter had suggested, but they are all still falling.

"Something tells me that isn't going to work. Also, where in the world are we supposed to get gas masks right now?" She jabs sarcastically at Hunter's ridiculous comment.

"Well, I don't see you coming up with any bright ideas," he shoots back.

He runs a hand through his curly hair. "ARGH!!!" Hunter cries out with a mixture of frustration, grief, and fear before turning toward the kitchen and punching a hole through the wall.

Jonah begins yelling at Hunter, and Clare screams at them to both stop arguing. However, Brooke remains silent, mesmerized by the world outside as the streets become desolate from hordes of falling bodies.

THE VIRUS SPREADS

Particles of large and strangely-colored dust gently dwindle from the dark sky, filling the boot-shaped tracks along the thin desert sand. The tracks lead to a young girl shuffling along through the piles left lying amongst the dunes, singing to herself and feeling a strange tickle across her rosy cheeks.

She had been in the hospital the past couple weeks for her schizophrenia and is blissfully unaware of the happenings occurring in the world as she trudges her way back home through the cover of nightfall.

She arrives at the back gates of her house and, to her surprise, steps in something wet and cold that she has never experienced before, especially in the middle of a desert. She continues to make her way to the back door, calling out to her parents as she steps inside and turns on the dim light.

"Mom! Dad! I'm home! Is there any dinner left?"

Silence answers. She can visibly see light coming from the living room to her left, but nobody is in sight.

That's weird. She thinks to herself as she sets her backpack down, the name "Chloe" stitched onto the front patch, on the kitchen table and takes off her unlaced boots, smoothing out her black socks as she does so.

The house feels somewhat cold, oddly cold, the feeling that something terrible had just happened.

"Dad! Are you home? Mom!"

More silence.

Maybe they ran out to the store? The fridge does look pretty bare.

Chloe shrugs as she pulls out a small container of pasta salad and begins picking at it.

A sudden *BANG* from the front of the house soon makes her jump and drop the container, pasta salad spilling out of the container and all over the tiled floor.

"Great. Just great..." Chloe mumbles to herself as she grabs a roll of paper towels. "Mom! Is that you? Dad?"

However, rather than comforting and familiar voices, she is again met with silence and an icy breeze.

Chloe stops short and freezes, kneeling onto the ground to pick up her mess.

Where is this breeze coming from? It's like 90 degrees right now.

She slowly rises and tiptoes out of the kitchen to throw the only remaining food in the house into the garbage bin, stopping when she sees the front door wide open.

Shit, who the hell is in my house?

"Mom!? Dad!?" As Chloe moves closer toward the front door, she notices that the screen door has been unhinged at the mercy of the night breeze.

"Dad! This isn't funny anymore. I'm scared and hungry," Chloe runs to the door to slam it shut, briefly remembering how her father would always prank her as a distraction from her hallucinations.

However, just as she is about to close the main door, the flickering porch lights catch her eyes, illuminating the ground outside, and exposing something dark and eerie on the steps. Still, Chloe struggles to make out what it is, some sort of dark puddle, too thick to be water from the rain or any source of water for that matter.

Cautiously and curiously, she steps outside and onto the top step, hugging her arms close to her body in fear.

No, it can't be. What is this? What the hell is this? And why does it smell like death?

Just before Chloe runs back inside the house from disgust, she notices something small and shiny sticking out from the middle of the black puddle. Quivering, she pinches her nostrils with her fingers and leans over the puddle to take a closer look. A piece of jewelry, a ring, from the looks of it.

Wait...mom?

Her mother's distinctive antique wedding ring is floating in the substance, with something that resembles a finger floating beside it.

"No! No, it's not real! This isn't real! It's not! Mom! Dad! You can't be gone! You can't! Come back! Come back..."

Her scream turns to jolted sobs that shake her entire body. Panicking at the unknown, she sprints away from her home, away from her mother, away from what else is lurking inside.

Glistening shards continue to drift down from the sky, dissolving in the black substance, covering the wedding ring as the remaining finger shatters into dust.

BE CAREFUL WHO YOU TRUST

"What the hell is that?" Jonah jumps from his seat as he leans forward to look closer at the human remains falling against the window. "This is really fucking creepy."

Clare looks up from her phone and watches as more mystifying chunks fall to the ground. They are...beige? Or maybe closer to a pale pink?

Brooke huddles closer, her blonde hair draping over Clare's shoulder. Hunter starts ranting nonsense to his live feed in the background as he browses the Internet, trying to find some more recent coverage that will let him know his impending fate. He needs to find out what's happening to the rest of the world, if they had figured out how to stop this monstrosity yet.

One hand tugs anxiously at his dark curls. His other hand shakes as he types on his laptop, eyes wide as he exaggerates the intensity of the situation to his fellow followers. Tears shine and threaten to fall as he sees picture after picture of black covered sand and grass, refusing to look away even as the girls speak about the falling debris. That is, not until he comes across a local report that has him running to a garbage can and throwing up his dinner.

"What is it?" Clare asks as she walks over to the laptop, playing the video that Hunter had just been watching.

She watches as the camera zooms in on a plane plummeting toward the ground. The plane plunges through the air, closer and closer to impact, the nose dipping at a greater angle with each passing moment.

The camera closes in on the front of the plane, and Clare can see that there is no pilot in the cockpit. The emergency doors and windows fling open, and strangely-colored material billows from every gaping orifice.

Wait a second...are those dust particles?

Clare squints closer at the video. A lake comes into view. It looks eerily similar to the lake that is a half mile away from the mansion they are currently in, along with a row of houses that look just like...

CRASH!

The world around them shakes as they watch the plane crash straight into the neighborhood lake. No, it most definitely is not dust particles falling outside. It is the remains, the fragmented pieces, of the people on the plane who had been infected with the disease.

Now, those human pieces coat the ground outside, the front porch, the roof, and even sticks onto the windowsills of the mansion. Jonah runs to take Hunter's place at the garbage can when he witnesses a small speck of blood-coated fingernail, the sound of his retching filling the room.

Oh, God. Clare runs to the front entryway and kneels to the ground.

Sure enough, tiny flakes of what had once been human flesh are being blown inside under the Victorian-style doors by the frigid breeze. She jumps up and barks at Brooke to follow her, who very much looks like she would rather take her turn hurling in the garbage can.

Clare drags her along anyway and starts to gather coats, shirts, towels – anything they can use to cram into the gaps between the floors and the doorways leading outside as she feels a sudden breeze coming through to the inside. She quickly sends Brooke to the back of the house while she deals with the front.

Before, she thought that would be an optional precaution; now, these flimsy fibers seem like the only barrier left between them and a lethal virus. And its aftermath.

"We need to cover the windows. NOW!" She orders those around her as she rushes past Jonah and Hunter with towels in hand.

She turns to check if they had heard her, but stops short at what she witnesses. The pair is holding each other in a tight embrace; Jonah, with his face buried in Hunter's shoulder, Hunter tugging at his own hair. Clare rolls her eyes and turns back to the window.

No, that's okay, she thinks bitterly, *I'll just barricade everything myself. While I'm at it, I'll just defeat the virus and save the whole planet, too! Freaking ridic—*

WHAM!

Clare shrieks as something large slams against the window she is attempting to cover. She stumbles back, falling to the floor, and for the first time that night, she feels a true surge of panic.

Pressed up against the window is Chloe, confused and afraid of the world shifting around her. Viewing the group inside, she begins clawing at the windows vigorously and pounding the glass with her fists, screaming incoherently.

Though her eyes are still intact, there are thin trails of blood seeping from her tear ducts. She sobs loudly as she continues to kick and thrash against the window.

"LET ME IN! LET ME IN! They're coming for me! Let me in!" Chloe repeatedly pounds against the window, close to shattering it if it hadn't been for the tempered glass.

Brooke rushes forward and cries desperately, "We have to help her!"

"NO!" Hunter catches Brooke's arm as she runs by and wraps her up in his own, pinning her against himself. "No, Brooke, we can't! It's too late. She'll just expose us! We can't save her..."

Brooke struggles against his grip as her own tears stream down her face.

"Clare! Clare, DO SOMETHING! She's just a kid! You have to help her, Clare, PLEASE!"

However, Clare remains frozen on the ground, staring at the girl on the other side of the glass, mouth hanging open, blood streaming down her face, hardly breathing.

Terrified.

Strangely enough, Chloe doesn't have the same midnight substance spewing out from her eye sockets. She isn't shattering like everyone else when she should be by now. She's just afraid, tears pouring out of her eyes as she continues to beg her way into the house.

"I...I...can't," Clare responds with shame and guilt while listening to Chloe's pleading cry.

"HELP ME! HELP ME!" Chloe continues to pound as a crowd of the infected comes rushing toward her. "Don't let them get me! Don't let them get me! PLEASE!!"

"I can't look!" Brooke exclaims as she turns her eyes away from the window and hides her face.

Clare freezes in disbelief as she witnesses the zombie-like crowd surround the girl and consume her, flashes shining through the clusters of people as the girl continues to scream. All Clare can do is squeeze her eyes shut and pray that the nightmare will soon be over.

Seconds later, the crowd shatters into smithereens, one by one, and Chloe is left lifeless on the ground, the midnight substance covering her limp body.

Oh my god. She's dead. And it's all my fault. I killed that girl. I should have let her in. Why the fuck didn't I just let her in??!

Clare turns her head away from the scene of the crime, her conscience eating away at her mind. When this chaos first began, she was able to separate herself from the monsters, the non-humans lurking the dilapidated Earth, from the civilized beings like herself. Now, she isn't so sure.

LOVE, GUILT, & DECEPTION

Clare pants, curled up in a small corner of the living room, staring at the mess she had just made and replaying what she had just seen in her mind. The girl. Her screams. Her eyes. As hard as she tries, Clare cannot push the image of the girl's scared and bleeding eyes out of her thoughts.

She was different, not like the rest of them. She didn't expel the same black substance as everyone else. She also didn't shatter, simply collapsing onto the ground instead. Who was she? What was she? Was she just human? Did I really just let an innocent human being die?

With the virus having been the norm, witnessing something normal becomes an anomaly, and that doesn't sit well with Clare. Maybe it's another unknown, an exception to the rules of the virus, which can only mean that things would get worse.

She hasn't felt this kind of adrenaline-soaked fear in a long time, possibly ever. It is overwhelming, as she keels over the small bucket beside her and hurls.

Clare cannot bring herself to stand up yet so she shifts to the right, bringing her face away from the vomit monstrosity on the shaggy carpet. She can feel the buzz of panic coursing through her veins, tickling her limbs, and forcing her heartbeat to race.

She shudders involuntarily, then feels the tiniest pinprick in her eye. She rubs it absentmindedly, then freezes when she draws her hand back – is that a trace of the black substance on her finger?

No, no, no... She breathes deeply, slowly, willing her pulse to decrease.

She drops her head to her hands, eyes closed, and tries to empty her mind of all feelings of guilt and sadness she continues to experience fear. It is a practice she had mastered over the years, thanks to her tragic childhood, and for the first time in her life, she is grateful for it. She lifts her head and touches her fingers to her eye once more.

Nothing.

Clare lets out a sigh of relief, her head falling back into her hands.

"Hey, are you doing okay over there?" Hunter yells from across the room.

Brooke had passed out amid the chaos and, naturally, Hunter is right at her side to help.

I swear there's something going on between those two. He better not fucking do anything with her.

Clare watches intensely as Hunter cradles Brooke's head in his lap and gently fans her face with his handkerchief, looking quizzically at Clare.

Clare nods as she starts to slowly raise herself up to all fours, keeping her thoughts to herself for the fear of letting her emotions spill through her eyes again.

"Yeah, I think so. Where's Jonah?"

As if on cue, the grating sound of a man retching echoes from the kitchen around the corner.

Hunter jerks his head toward the sound and raises his eyebrows. It is then that Clare notices he is covered in a sheen of sweat.

"That was a rough one for all of us, but especially him."

Clare nods in agreement and pushes herself up to her knees. "She didn't seize, Hunter."

He pauses, then shakes his head, "You don't know that. It all happened so fast. She probably did, but you just didn't see it."

"No, I'm telling you, she didn't seize. She was shaking, but she didn't convulse like the others. She didn't bleed like the others. Why was that? Why was she different?"

Before Hunter can respond, Brooke raises her head from Hunter's lap.

She groans, "Jonah...Hunter? Clare?"

"Yeah, Brooke. I'm here. We're here," Hunter smiles down at her while Clare crawls over to join them, grasping Hunter's hand.

Brooke breathes in a deep sigh, "Oh my God, I don't know what happened. My body just shut down, and the next thing I know, I'm on the floor. The last thing I remember seeing was..." her voice trails off as her eyes shift to the window.

Blood still speckled on the glass.

Brooke's voice drops to a whisper, "So, I guess she—"

Clare presses her lips together and nods. Hunter clears his throat uncomfortably.

Just as Hunter begins to speak, the loud bang of a falling trashcan disrupts their train of thought. The trio turns to see Jonah standing in the doorway between the kitchen and the living room. His eyes are puffy from crying, his nose is bright red, and his top lip looks swollen, as if he had been chewing on it.

He clutches a paper towel in one hand and his phone in the other. There is a slight tremble to his entire body, even as his gaze remains steady. His usually perfect locks had become a hot mess, with wisps of hair falling onto his face, and a small stain appears near the collar of his shirt.

"She died," he states as he walks toward them. "Just say it. She died right there, and we couldn't help her. She was young. She didn't deserve it. God knows where her family is or if they're looking for her, if they're even alive themselves."

He steps further into the living room. "We can't even help a little kid when she's all alone and scared out of her mind?! This is bullshit! It's not human!"

Infuriated, Jonah smashes his fist into the wall beside him and creates a fairly large hole. Shocked, the other three do not quite know what to say so they just stare at him as he continues to slowly move closer to them.

"I am here, and my little brother is home. Do you know who I want to be with during some fucking pandemic, more than anyone in the world? My little brother!" He holds up his phone for emphasis, trembling.

"My brother! Not you people! But no, I can't be with my brother. Because I came here. I came to this goddam party instead of staying home...because of you, Brooke. So, thanks for that. Thanks for keeping me trapped inside a house that isn't mine, while my brother is sitting at home, all alone, without me. Thanks for taking me AWAY FROM HIM!" He screams and lunges for Brooke who tries to back away from Jonah's terrifying scream.

Clare cries out and tackles Jonah to the side. Hunter yells and flings himself over Brooke like a human shield as Brooke covers her face with her palms and cries, everyone yelling at each other all at once.

"Stop it! Stop, Jonah, it's not her fault! You know it isn't!" Clare insists as she presses Jonah's arms to the ground.

"I'm sorry! I didn't know! I'm so sorry! You have to believe me, I'm sorry!" Brooke wails, wrapping her long arms around Hunter's waist.

"You're being ridiculous! Calm down! I said, calm down, Jonah!" Hunter calls out to the man pierced against the carpet as he holds Brooke closer to his chest.

"I can't! I can't calm down! My brother needs me! I need my little bro! I need my bro! I need—" Jonah breaks down into violent sobs in Clare's arms. He clings desperately to Clare and buries his face in her shoulders as his own shoulders heave.

Brooke sits up from Hunter's lap and crawls over, wrapping her arms around Jonah and crying softly with her friend. "I know, I need my family too. I need them too. I'm sorry, Jonah, I'm sorry..."

Clare looks over their heads at Hunter, a glimmer of tears shine in her eyes for the first time that night.

Hunter shakes his head, "We can't afford to turn on each other like that. This virus is enough of an enemy."

Clare purses her lips into a grim line as she pulls her hair back into a ponytail. She can barely get her voice above a whisper, "Maybe that's how it starts."

IGNORANCE OF THE INFECTED

Isabella Robinson stands outside in the gray of early dawn, shivering, partly from the frigid wind, but largely due to horror. This has been the hardest day of her reporting career – no, of her life. She has never felt so helpless.

There are thousands of reports streaming in from this county alone, millions of reports from the state. She is afraid to find out what's going on in the rest of the world.

Every national channel shows footage of the same thing happening all over the world: airports in chaos with jet planes plunging from the sky, trains colliding together with no engineers to stop them, dozens of puddles of blood staining the ground, and sparkling flakes fluttering though the air in place of where a human being had once stood. She needs to get as much information as she possibly can about this incident.

"Excuse me! Excuse me, miss! Can I get a moment of your time?!" Isabella asks as she approaches a group of girls standing in front of a coffee shop.

However, they are too busy posting their many selfies on Centriclist to acknowledge her.

"Oh my god! Can you believe she's going out with him? What a slut!" One of the girls remark.

"Excuse me, sir! Sir! Can I speak with you for a moment?" Isabella asks a man sitting on a small patch of grass, feeding sunflower seeds to his dog and dressing him up as a bumblebee.

"Sure thing, lovely lady. Feel free to ask me anything about my dazzling self," The man egotistically replies.

"What is your name, sir?" Isabella questions the man.

"Davith is the name. Don't wear it out," the man responds as he winks at Isabella.

"Uh...Davith. What are your thoughts to what's going on around us? What do you think is happening to people? Do you believe in the rumor that taking selfies is the cause of the spread of this deadly and strange virus?"

"What?! That's preposterous! No way can something as fucking amazing as taking pictures of my gorgeous self cause something like this. It's probably just a bug going around. Nothing I need to concern myself with. I'm in impeccable shape!" Davith replies as he snaps an image of himself, shirt unbuttoned.

"You're not afraid that your picture will cause you to catch the virus?"

"Nah, the only thing I'm concerned about is whether I can get 500,000 likes from this sick post!"

"Thank you for your time, Davith," Isabella nervously says as she slowly backs away from him.

Sheesh, what an ego on that man. Let's see if I can find someone else. Someone more normal.

Isabella spots a group of single mothers with their baby carriages standing by the produce stand and approaches them to see if they can give her some decent answers.

"Excuse me, miss!" Isabella shouts as she approaches the woman closest to her.

However, she is met with no response, not even a twitch when her hand touches the shoulder.

"Miss?"

Isabella turns the woman around and drops her mic as she sees the eyes of the woman liquefying beyond belief.

She had known that this was happening, but never did she think she would come face-to-face with death. It is horrifying, gory, so grotesque that Isabella almost throws up in her mouth upon seeing the woman. She hurriedly turns around the remaining three women and, not only are they all liquefying the midnight substance from their eyes, but so are their babies.

One by one, the midnight-colored substance consumes them as they shatter and vanish into thin air, causing Isabella to fall onto the ground from the shock.

"You okay, Is?" Joey, her cameraman, comes up to her, helping her off the ground.

"Yeah...yeah. Just...surprised, that's all. Did you find anyone who fits our profile?" Isabella asks.

"No, not yet, but I was j-just thinking. It's not...n-not looking too good. Can I use your phone? Please? I'd like to call m-my, my w-wife," Joey chokes back a soft sob with these last words.

"Oh, of course, Joey," Isabella fishes in her coat pocket for her phone.

She sadly looks at him with tears trickling from the corners of her eyes. "Take all the time you need, okay?"

He nods his thanks and takes a couple steps away as he dials.

Isabella turns and looks back at the Channel 6 News building. The production crew and anchors have barricaded themselves inside when the spread of the virus surged, locking out Isabella and her reporting crew, people they had known and worked with for over 10 years.

Sick, she thinks.

But, then again, part of her can't blame them. If she had the choice of either risking her life to help an infected co-worker or saving her own skin, she would have chosen the latter also. People love to say that they would bravely lay down their lives for their fellow men, but only when the sun is shining and the threat of danger is merely a myth.

When the sky darkens and that fated moment comes knocking at the door, the sentiment of good will and faith evaporate and are replaced by the primordial need for survival.

She sighs deeply as she listens to Joey speak into the phone. She had called her husband a couple of hours ago, with no answer, too afraid to call again since. Which is more difficult to face: another missed call, or a call answered, just to listen to the virus take hold of another?

She shakes her head and swallows the lump in her throat. She must stay focused; this is her job. More than that, this is her calling. She needs the world to know and acknowledge this story. She needs to keep her viewers informed of the danger for as long as she possibly can.

Joey comes shuffling back over, sniffling, and hands back her phone. "Thanks. I needed that."

Isabella nods. "How is she doing? Everything okay?"

Joey shakes his head, "Aw, there was no answer, so I left her a message."

"You...you left her a message?"

He attempts to smile, "Yeah, I know it sounds silly, leaving a message for someone who may potentially be gone already, but I had to. I had to tell her one last time how much I love her and miss her. Even though she probably won't..." he stops and clears his throat. "...she probably won't get it – I'm just being honest with myself – I'd like to believe that wherever she is, she can still hear my voice."

Isabella smiles sorrowfully, "Yeah, Joey. I think she does. I'll be right back, okay?"

As Joey nods, she takes a few steps away and faces the slowly rising sun. Inhaling deeply, Isabella presses the name on her contact list: Ryan.

The phone rings once...twice...three times. Tears start to gather in her eyes. She knows what that means; she can feel it in her bones, but still she waits.

The phone rings a final time, then a pre-recorded voice comes through the speaker, "Hey! This is Ryan, sorry I missed you. Drop me a message after the thing beeps. And if you're selling something, let me save you some time – not interested, and please put me on the 'Do Not Call' list. See ya!"

Isabella sniffs as a beep sounds, "Hey, it's me. Um...obviously, things are not good. I'm sure you've...seen and heard. Hopefully from a distance. But...I just called to say that I—" her voice catches in her throat. "Sorry, I... I really love you, Ryan. I love you, and I would give anything in the world to say that to your face right now, but...here we are. Um, I just hope that you knew that. Uh, know that, rather. And I..."

She closes her eyes and lets out a shaky breath. "I'll...I'll see you soon, Ry."

She lowers the phone from her ear and lets a few tears roll down her face. The sun is peeking over the horizon now, and she can feel the warmth start to cut through the chill of the storm. The end is near. She knows that.

Deep down, she knows that they had all been doomed from the start. This disease, or whatever it is, came out of nowhere, too vicious and powerful for anyone to react, let alone escape.

The word "unprecedented" seems too sterile of a word to use when there are masses of people literally shattering on the streets.

Through her tears, she can feel a tiny prick of pain in her eye, and her fingers instinctually fly toward her face. They come back with the clear fluid of her tears, laced with the smallest traces of midnight.

Without taking her eyes off her hand, Isabella calls back to her crew, "We need to broadcast, NOW!"

No response. She turns around.

Her crew gathers together, their backs to Isabella, stammering and looking down at the puddle in front of them. She can feel the pit in her stomach growing as she runs over to the group and pushes her way to the front. Shock overtakes her body, and she stumbles back into the arms of her audio technician when she sees what they are gawking at.

Joey, the sweetest man she has ever worked with, kneels on the ground before them. His eyes seem to have dissolved, and streams of the black substance pour from the sockets where they had once been. Cracks begin forming along his skin, making his face look like fractured desert terrain.

Despite this, Joey is still smiling. He shakes and quivers as the cracks grow and the blood pours, but his smile remains still. He wraps his arms around himself and falls backwards, facing upwards toward the sky. With one short-lived groan, his body shatters into thousands of tiny pieces, leaving the midnight liquid in the sand and glittering flakes in the air.

Isabella sinks to her knees and lets her tears fall freely. Her photographer wretches. Her makeup artist whimpers, staring at the spot where Joey had just been.

Her audio technician covers his face and repeats, "Oh my God, oh my God..."

Isabella feels the sting in her eye again, this time, a little more prominent. She wipes it with the back of her hand and inspects her fingers – black.

"We need to broadcast. NOW!" She says decisively once again.

"But...we don't have a cameraman," the photographer protests.

Isabella holds up her phone and offers a weak smile, "Sure we do."

JONAH'S BREAKING POINT

Hours pass as Clare flicks through television stations. Each new broadcast becomes more gruesome than the last, with people dying left and right. It looks like there will never be an end in sight, never mind any time soon. More hours, more people dying.

Clare doesn't remember when the sun had risen, but sure enough, the sun is peeking over the horizon and illuminating the room through the thin towels the group had used to cover the windows.

She moves one aside as she sits on the window seat and surveys the world outside. The rays of morning light glisten on the blood-covered hills, tranquil and beautiful, almost as if the world isn't coming to a catastrophic end.

"I need to try to get home," Jonah murmurs as he looks out the window over Clare's shoulder. "My brother and I have been texting all night. He thinks that now it's safe enough for me to try, and he's going to meet me halfway. He said we can probably make it down the road and get inside before the disease takes hold."

Clare's mouth drops open before snapping shut again. "Are you kidding me? Are you and your brother completely stupid? Do you have a death wish that you failed to tell us about? In case you forgot, Jonah, we already lost most of the influencers last night. Why do you want to add yourself to that list?"

Tears trickle down Jonah's face once more as he buries it in his hands.

"I just want to go home and hug my little brother one last time. This could be the end either way! We don't know what's going to happen today, or tomorrow, or the next day. If I'm going to die, I want it to be at home, with him. Is that so wrong?"

Hunter's laptop screeches as a local broadcast overpowers the one they had been watching on the television. Instead of a professional camera taping the scene, the reporter is holding her phone in front of her. The quality of the video is grainy and bleak. She has black trails streaming down her cheeks as normal tears turn dark.

"I'm afraid that this may be my final broadcast. We have been monitoring this terrible pandemic throughout the night, and now we have just received information regarding a disastrous break in this lethal virus' trend.

Francesca Lauren, age thirty-five, has died in her home due to this mysterious disease. Her neighbor in the apartment next door heard her screams and ran over to help, only to find her convulsing in bed just moments before she shattered. This incident has confirmed that the virus cannot be avoided by remaining isolated. It will find you, and it will kill you."

She takes a shaky breath, then continues, "I wish that I could tell you all a different story. I wish that there is a glimmer of hope for us all to cling onto. Sadly, there is not. As a reporter, I am obligated to stick to the facts, so here they are.

Hug your loved ones. Hold onto them tightly for as long as this virus will allow you to, and keep each other close in these final moments. It has been an honor and a pleasure to bring you our area's top local news coverage, even in these times of darkness. Signing off for the last time, I'm Isabella Robinson, Channel 6 News."

At that moment, the phone careens into a freefall, landing on the ground beside the reporter. Her convulsions can be clearly seen as the blackness pours from her eyes. Then, just like that, she is gone, nothing more than shattered pieces scattering along the ground.

A trembling hand reaches down and grabs the phone seconds before the screen turns dark.

"I'm going to go," Jonah stammers as he stares at the door. "If I'm going to die, I want it to be on my own terms. At my house, with my brother."

Clare snaps her head to stare incredulously at Jonah. She shakes her head, her eyes stinging. "Are you insane, Jonah? You can't do that; you won't last long enough to get there."

Brooke stands next to Jonah and places a hand on his shoulder. "Are you afraid?" She asks softly.

Jonah nods as more tears pour fresh. "Yeah, but I don't want to die without a choice in the matter."

Hunter pipes up from behind them, "Uh, guys?" He points out the window.

The influencers turn to see what he is talking about. Across the street, someone is stumbling toward the mansion, his face completely shrouded by a blanket he had wrapped around his head. His arms are outstretched, but every so often, they would reach up to his face to separate the folds of the blanket, enough to see where his steps are taking him. The light coat of skin on his face is freckled with bloodstains, but he keeps pushing forward.

All of a sudden, he trips over the pavement and falls to his hands and knees. The blanket drops from his head.

Jonah gasps, "That's my brother!"

Jonah's brother has trails of the substance running down his face, but his eyes remain intact. He is shaking so terrifyingly that it is impossible for him to stand again. He looks up and sees the group gathered at the window.

Grimacing in pain, he raises a quivering hand, reaching out to the house, reaching out for his brother.

Jonah lets out a cry and pulls away from Brooke, flinging himself out the front door before anyone can stop him. He slams it shut and runs across the street to his brother, barefoot, no coat to speak of despite the chilling wind, rushing to be at his brother's side.

However, before he can get there, he stumbles. The virus had claimed him too. Dark trails pour from his eyes, and those remaining can hear him groaning in pain even from inside the house. His legs completely useless, Jonah's brother pulls himself along the street toward Jonah, fixated on reaching his big brother.

Jonah falls to the ground, the trails turning to full rivers of darkness. Still, he persists, half-standing, half-crawling, desperate to hug his brother one last time.

Jonah sobs, holding his stomach as he doubles over. Hunter stands at the window, banging on it with his fist and shouting. Clare watches from further away, her whole body shaking, her breath coming in gasps.
The two of them are so close! Only a few more steps!

Just as their hands touch – they both shatter.

The fragments of their bodies seem to intermingle together, suspended in the air for only a short moment, before the breeze carries them away.

HOPELESS SALVATION

National Center for Emerging and Zoonotic Infectious Diseases

"Sir? We've obtained a sample."

A virologist raises his head from a microscope. His thin-framed glasses perch delicately on an impressive nose. His thin wisps of gray hair are gelled down to his head, and age spots are beginning to show themselves along his skin.

His name is Dr. Conner. He is the Chief Researcher for the viral division of the Center for Disease Control, and this has been the most difficult day of his scientific career.

"Excellent. Thank you, Mark."

He hurries over to his assistant researcher who had come bolting into the lab. The young man holds an evidence bag in his hand. An unorthodox means of transporting a specimen, but they find themselves in a rather unorthodox time in history. He gingerly lifts the sealed bag and holds it up toward the light.

Inside is a shred of clothing soaked in the black substance that has been plaguing everyone in the country, surrounded by a dozen glass-like fragments.

He turns back to his assistant, "Well. Let's save humanity, shall we?"

The two men set the evidence bag inside a sterile container. They walk over to one of the many supply cabinets found within the laboratory and pull out two hazmat suits. After donning their protective equipment, they take the specimen bag into a sealed cube that is completely sterile and filled with the purest filtered air technology can produce.

They open the bag. Dr. Conner holds up his hand, signaling a pause. They wait and look at each other to see if anything happens, paying special attention to the eyes.

Nothing changes.

They breathe a small sigh of relief and continue to unpack the precious sample. This is the first time they have managed to get their hands on the mysterious disease.

Being able to analyze and study it could potentially lead to a vaccine, an antidote, a cure...but really, any information at all would be wildly helpful at this point.

They get right to work. First, they extract as much of the substance from the piece of cloth as they can. They then run the matter through a centrifuge so they can isolate the particles containing the virus.

Next, they separate the glassy fragments from each other and place each one in its own petri dish of a dissolving solution. If this truly is a virus, as it is believed to be, they will be able to identify its antibodies after a few simple tests.

The first test fails to produce any results.

So does the second, and the third, and the fourth...

They run test after test, adjusting and tweaking their methods, until they believe themselves to be crazy – there is no presence of viral antibodies to be found. All their results are inconclusive.

Dr. Conner sinks into a chair in the corner of the room. He doesn't understand. He is the best in his field, has been for years, and he has been the sole player in ending every major pandemic in his professional lifetime.

Except this one. He can't seem to find the answer. But it HAS to be there, it just HAS to be! With his luck, it is probably staring him right in the face, but he is too blind to see it.

"Sir?" Mark speaks with a slight quiver in his voice.

He has never seen the doctor look so defeated. It isn't a comforting sight.

Dr. Conner looks up. "I don't know what it is, Mark."

"What? No, maybe we don't know what it is right now. We just have to keep testing. We just have to keep trying!"

"No!" Dr. Conner slams his fist down on the table next to him. "Don't you get it? I don't know what it is! I don't know what this stupid bug is that's killing millions of people worldwide. I don't know how to stop it!"

He stands up and starts pacing the room. "It's not a virus, or anything, that we have heard of, we know that much. It's not an airborne bacterium. It's not a fungal infection. It's not an environmental anomaly, it's—" he stops as he realizes the gravity of what he is about to say: "It's nothing like we've ever seen before."

Mark's jaw hangs open, but he starts to shake his head in protest.

"No. No, sir, we just have to keep exploring; there has to be an answer. There's always an answer!"

"Well, kid, this time there isn't!" Dr. Conner roars.

Mark falls quiet. He pensively asks, "Well, then...what do we do?"

Dr. Conner wonders that as well. What to do, indeed. They are the top scientists in the country, probably the world, and they have no answer as to how to stop this mad disease. He stands up suddenly and heads toward the exit. "Come," he says to Mark. "We have to make a call."

The two men exit the cube safely, leaving all traces of the diseased pieces behind them in the quarantine room. They strip their hazmat suits off and dump them in the appropriate bin, then Dr. Conner makes his way to a red landline phone that hangs in the corner by the doorway to the lab. He lays his hand on it and pauses for a moment, thinking hard.

Is there any other solution?

With a strong "Ahem!" and a shake of his shoulders, he picks up the receiver and presses 1. The line rings twice before a female's shaky voice answers.

"H-Hello?"

"Haley? Hello, it's Dr. Conner. I need...I need the President on the line, please."

A sob comes through the earpiece of the phone. "I'm sorry, Dr. Conner. The President is...well, he's gone, sir."

Dr. Conner pinches his nose between his thumb and forefinger. "You mean he went outside when he knew the potential consequences?"

"N-n-no, sir. No, he didn't go outside. He was sitting right here, just right here! Oh, it's awful, it's just awful..."

The Doctor freezes. His breathing becomes very heavy. "Haley? Haley, say that again. Did you say that the President was inside, with no contact made with the outside air, when this incident occurred?"

"What?!" Mark rushes to the Doctor's side, incredulous.

Haley tearfully confirms that this was indeed the case.

Shit, Dr. Conner slams the telephone receiver against the wall. "Okay, then get me the Vice President. Can I please speak to him, Haley?"

Haley only wails on the other end.

"Haley, am I correct in assuming that the Vice President is no longer with us either?" His tone becomes increasingly panicked. "Listen to me, sweetheart. Please answer this as best you can: how many people are over there with you?"

"It's...it's just, just me, sir."

Dr. Conner's face turns pale. He slowly hangs up the phone as Haley continues to whimper on the other end. He turns to his assistant, Mark.

"Son, you should call your family right away. We're all at risk, no matter how far indoors we may be."

Mark recoils when the doctor turns. He continues to back away, pointing at Dr. Conner's face, his mouth opening and closing like a fish.

"What? What is it, Mark?" Dr. Conner asks.

But as soon as the words leave his mouth, he feels it. A stinging sensation in his eye. A hot wetness leaking from his eyelids. A sudden burning sensation that starts just behind his eyeballs, then spreads to his brain, then the back of his neck, then takes over his whole body.

"ARGHHHH!" The doctor wails in pain as he sinks to the floor, ripping at his clothes and clutching at his cranium.

The substance flows freely from his eyes now, soaking his shirt and pooling on the ground around him.

Everything goes black. He feels as if he is on fire. No, like someone had opened the top of his skull and is pouring molten steel into his body from the top down.

Mark falls to the ground as well, screaming as the darkness rushes down his cheeks. He writhes in anguish, convulsing as the seizures take over his entire being. Both men continue their twisted dance of agonized suffering until *POOF!* They shatter into millions of tiny pieces, scattering across the laboratory floor.

Silence descends upon the lab.

Then, echoing through the empty chamber, the red phone rings.

HUNTER'S SURRENDER

Clare madly searches through the Internet for any news, any updates, anybody speaking. Nothing. All that is on the web is dead air. There are no new reports, no hope being spread. This disease will surely kill them soon enough. Though it had been hard to watch Jonah and the others go, Clare finds an odd sense of comfort in knowing how she will die.

So much for going down in a blaze of glory, she thinks as she checks her phone.

The battery is completely dead. Clare quietly begins to cry as she realizes that she won't be able to say "goodbye" to her parents or sister. Maybe they still don't want to hear from her, if they are even still alive, but now, she will never get the opportunity to at least try to mend those broken fences.

All she truly wants in this moment is to go home to her family. Fuck rebellion. Fuck Centriclist. Fuck influencing. She just wants to go home.

Hunter clears his throat as he comes into the room. Clare is now stationed at the window seat and turns to face him with a sad smile. He crosses the room and stands, looking down at her with a softness in his eyes. His hand drifts up to cup Clare's jaw, a tender glimpse at the love they had both lusted over for years.

Clare's eyes close as she leans into Hunter's hand, turning her head slightly to press a kiss against his palm.

"I love you," Hunter whispers.

Clare squeezes her eyes tight, a smile playing at her lips. "I love you too, Hunt."

"But I can't live like this."

Clare jerks back. "What? Don't say that, Hunter! It's still early, we don't know what could happen!"

Hunter nods as Brooke walks into the room.

"Exactly. We don't know what could happen. It could get worse, much worse, and be more painful in the long run. And look at what's left after just one night! So many people, just gone. Our families, probably gone. Is it even worth it to survive?"

Tears are running down his face, but his voice remains strong.

Clare stands up and grabs his arms as she looks directly into Hunter's eyes.

"Of course, it's worth it to survive! What are you talking about? You just said it, you love me, and guess what? I freaking love you too. I hate that it took me until this moment to tell you, but I do, Hunter. Our love isn't just for fame and attention anymore. It's real. I don't care who knows it and who doesn't. I'll take care of you. I'll guard you. I would let this 'thing' take me a thousand times over before I let it get to you!"

Hunter laughs weakly at her grandiose promises.

"You can't say that. It's a virus, Clare. It doesn't pick and choose who its victims are. It can't listen to reason. It won't care if you throw yourself in front of me. It takes, and it kills. That simple."

With those words, Clare bursts out into tears.

She can only get her voice to a hoarse whisper, "Hunter, please. You're not serious. Please don't go out there. It would kill me."

Hunter shakes his head. "No, it wouldn't. The virus would kill you; it's going to kill all of us eventually. I just want to have a say in the matter when it takes me."

Clare wipes her eyes and watches her man.

"But what if they can come up with a cure?"

Hunter smiles and walks over to embrace her.

"Then do me a favor and take it. But I'm afraid, Clare. I don't want to live my whole life being afraid."

"Well, too bad, I need you here! Brooke needs you here!" Clare yells.

Hunter shakes his head. "I'm sorry, Clare."

"You're being selfish!"

"Maybe I am. But Clare, I'll always be in your heart, and you'll be in mine."

"I don't want you in my heart. I want you here with me, damn it!"

Clare breaks down into sobs and flings herself at Hunter. The two lovers hug tightly, crying together. Brooke turns away and buries her own tear-stained face in her hands. It is too much to bear.

After what seems like forever, Hunter pulls back. He cups Clare's face in his hands.

"You're the greatest girlfriend a man could ever have. But I need to go. This is killing me just sitting and waiting. You understand, don't you?"

Clare sniffles, "Wait." She runs into the kitchen and re-emerges a couple of moments later, holding three disposable plastic cups and the pitcher of the mysterious cocktail Jonah had mixed for the party.

Hunter laughs and wipes her face as he accepts the cup from Clare. Even Brooke manages to crack a small grin.

Clare pours a hefty amount into each of their cups, then raises her own in the air.

She says in a trembling voice, "To Hell: may the stay there be as enjoyable as the way there."

Hell. What once seemed like a mythical place feels all too tangible in these moments. The three influencers raise their glasses. Then, looking around at each other, they all start to cry together. They can't help it. It is all too absurd. It is all too unbelievable, the situation they are finding themselves in. It is all too real.

Silently, Hunter gathers the cups from everyone so he can say his last farewells. He throws his arms around Clare and squeezes her harder than he had squeezed anyone in his life.

"You stay here as long as you can, okay?" he whispers into Clare's ear.

Clare can only nod through the sobs that choke her throat.

Hunter walks over to the door as Brooke moves to Clare's side. The two remaining influencers cling to each other for support, in every sense of the word. Hunter pauses with his hand resting on the doorknob. He turns once more to them and silently raises his hand in a resolute wave.

He walks out the door.

Clare runs over to the window. She screams as she watches the disease take her lover, bargaining everything she has with some unseen deity. Brooke sinks to her knees on the carpet, with violent sobs racking her entire body.

THE END OF AN ERA

Clare isn't sure how long it has been. Had hours passed? Had minutes? Maybe even days? It feels like a lifetime ago when she witnessed her boyfriend give himself up to the virus, too afraid and too exhausted to fight anymore.

Clare has been a wreck ever since that moment, spending all her time pacing between the living room and the kitchen, tugging at her curls, chewing on her lip. Her eyes are vacant.

Every time Brooke tries to speak to her, it is as if she can't even hear her. Instead, she goes upstairs to an old bedroom and curls up in the queen-sized bed, shaking with soft sobs as she holds a photo of Hunter in her hand. Brooke, finding it best to leave Clare alone in her grief, remains downstairs and processes her own heartache.

Brooke sighs and shifts her position on the window seat. She lies in a fetal position, hugging herself, desperate to fabricate any form of comfort that she can.

She closes her eyes and tries to sleep for the first time since everything started, but it is still an impossible task. Any time she closes her eyes, all she sees are dark pools of sludge on the streets, flesh-colored flakes falling from the sky, little girls pounding on the window, Todd and Kayla...Bill. Her eyes open again. She can't relive that yet. It is still too fresh, however long it has been since it happened.

She sits up and turns the TV on, flipping through the many channels of static and wondering how long it would be before another human comes back on the screen. It has been so long since the last report they saw from the Channel 6 news lady. Isn't there anyone who can tell them something? Anything?

As if on cue, one channel suddenly comes through with an actual picture. A reporter, sitting inside the back of a news van. Over his shoulder, you can see the White House in the background through the van window. Brooke comes closer to the screen and squints. So far, it looks like this guy hasn't been exposed.

The whites of his eyes are as white as his teeth, no blackness to be seen. His skin is perfectly smooth, no cracks, not even a blemish to speak of. He remains still and calm in front of the camera, even though his voice trembles slightly as he reads his report:

"Sources have confirmed that our esteemed President, Bryden Walters, has passed away. Members of the White House staff have reported that several of the people inside have suffered from the mysterious virus that is spreading throughout the world. Though it has not been confirmed, we have reason to believe that the President also suffered from this disease before his passing."

He pauses and holds a finger to his earpiece. His eyes widen, and his face drains of color just slightly. Gathering himself, he speaks again.

"My apologies, ladies and gentlemen. But we have also received exclusive breaking news that the Vice President, Mr. Luther Prayer, has also passed away due to complications from this virus. Officials are strongly advising everyone to remain indoors and secure all entry points to your home. These recent events may result in a high increase of domestic terrorism, so please, stay inside, and stay safe."

Brooke turns the stupid television off and throws the remote. How can this get any worse? Not only do they have to fear an invisible enemy in the virus, but now, they have to fear each other too. Who is safe anymore?

Curious, she turns the TV on again to the same channel, just in time to see the deadly black substance trickling down the reporter's cheeks, as he desperately dabs at it with a paper towel.

Figures. Brooke turns it off with a groan and vows never to watch the news again.

She hears a creak behind her and twists around to see that Clare had come down the stairs. She now stands in the entryway to the living room, staring at the ground. She is a mess. Her hair points in all different directions. Dark circles frame her eyes. Her face is distended from crying.

"Hey," Brooke speaks softly, as she feels an aching heartbreak for the devastated Clare. "How are you doing?"

Clare can only nod her head, her eyes still fixated on the floor in front of her.

"Do you want something to eat?"

She shakes her head this time.

"Do you want something to drink?"

Again, she shakes her head.

Brooke sighs, "How can I help you then, if you won't tell me what you want?"

Clare looks up for the first time in hours. "I just want him back, Brooke." Her voice sounds hoarse, making it even more heartbreaking to hear.

"I know...I'm sorry. I'm tired of this too." Brooke sympathizes as she places a hand on Clare's shoulder.

She waves her off, "No, it's okay. No one has a manual on how to handle these things anyway."

Brooke grins wryly. "It does hurt though. Hunter, I mean. It hurts me too."

Clare sniffs and looks back down at the floor, shuffling her feet. "Yeah, I know. Just my luck, right? Right when we profess our love to each other, this shit happens." She clears her throat and looks up at Brooke once more. "He was great, and he wouldn't want us to be sad about it. He made his choice."

Brooke nods. "Yeah, he did."

"And... you know, we all have to make our own choices when it comes to this, right?"

Brooke pauses, trying to decipher what she is saying, "What do you mean by that, Clare?"

Clare shakes her head. "Never mind, forget that I said anything."

She shuffles across the carpet to where Brooke is perched. She looks out the window, not seeing any people outside, whether they were walking, stumbling, or writhing. Only small patches of black-stained sand remain, the one thing indicating that the world is currently turning upside-down.

"Do you think it's calming down out there? I don't see anybody moving around."

Brooke shakes her head. "I don't think it's ever going to calm down. It's only going to get worse, and it's going to kill us all eventually. Hunter was right about that. Also, I've been thinking a lot about what he said, and I think I agree. I don't want this disease to kill me. It looks painful."

Clare stands and runs her hands through her hair.

"I have an idea. I know how we can make death not hurt and avoid letting the virus be the thing that takes us."

"What do you mean?"

She shakes her head, not answering, and leaves the room. When she returns, she is holding a small gun in one hand and two bullets in the other. Brooke's eyes widen as she realizes where her thoughts have gone. It has only been a few short days since the outbreak, and they had already lost their minds and gone insane.

"Clare, where the hell did you get that?"

"I always keep a gun with me, you know, with all the hitchhiking and everything. You never know what or who you might run into."

"Well, put it away!"

"What? No! Don't you see, Brooke? This is the only way! We don't want to die like everyone else did! We don't want to stick around and see what else could possibly explode in our faces! We want control, don't we? Well, this is it! This is control, right here!"

She waves the gun in the air.

Brooke isn't crying, but her breath catches in her throat like a sob.

"But this is crazy. This is suicide."

"Yeah, what would you call what Hunter did?" Clare shoots back.

Brooke sputters, "No, but that...but he...that was different!"

Clare shakes her head vehemently, "No, it's not, Brooke. And you know it's not. Hunter made his choice, and we have to make ours. This is my choice, this!"

She gingerly loads the two bullets into the chamber. "If you have any alternative plans, please, I would love to hear about them."

Brooke trembles as she stares at the gun in Clare's hands. What other options are there? Her friends are all gone. Her family is probably gone. Gone, gone, gone, gone...

Brooke squeezes her eyes shut and clasps her head in her hands. This is all too much. She shouldn't have to make this decision; it isn't fair! She shouldn't have to watch everyone that she ever cared about die a horrible death!

She shouldn't have to hide inside a house that isn't even her own, just waiting for some invisible monster to come in the night and steal her soul away! She shouldn't have to be scared. She shouldn't have to be gripped with terror at every moment. She is tired of wallowing in fear.

"I'm afraid, Clare. I don't want to be afraid anymore," Brooke cries, dampness tracking down her cheeks.

She raises her fingers, and they come away bloody. Her heart rate surges, and she knows that it is time. This is her answer. This is her choice. She turns an imploring look to Clare as the blood pours faster down her face.

"Please? Please just do it."

Clare takes a deep breath to steel herself and places the barrel against Brooke's forehead.

"No, wait. I don't want to be the last one to go. I want to be with Hunter as soon as I can. Here, take the gun. Put me out of my misery first."

Shaking, Brooke slowly opens her eyes from the fear of getting shot in the head and carefully pulls the gun away from Clare.

"I...I don't know if I can do this." She says anxiously.

"JUST DO IT!" Clare shouts with her eyes closed and hands in the air.

And with that, her body hits the floor. As Brooke turns the gun on herself, the television flickers.

X9Y9X

"Good evening, fellow survivors." A man on the screen announces.

"What?" Brooke questions to herself as she slowly lowers the gun, the blood of Clare still splattered on her face.

"As you all may have already figured out, there is a deadly virus going around that is causing the eyes of human beings to liquefy and their bodies to shatter into millions of glass shards. This virus is called X9Y9X and was developed by the United States in an attempt to stabilize the world, a world that is currently brainwashed by an ego so large that humans have only been able to focus on themselves and their own desires.

This virus was intended to stabilize the human ego by forcing us to deter from the use of selfies as a means of self-gratification.

However, there was a breach in the developing facility when the North Koreans infiltrated the lab, stealing the viral samples and altering it so the virus becomes much,

much more deadly. You may have noticed that only those who refrain from selfies and Centriclist become the sole survivors of this disease, the virus unable to attach onto them because their egos are not large enough for the connection.

This chaotic incident is not only happening in your town; it is global, a widespread pandemic that the North Koreans have inflicted upon the world, a massive scheme channeled to wipe out the shallow people of the world. The world around you is collapsing.

People are incinerating from their own shallow habits yet, still refuse to stop even as those around them are continuing to perish right before their very eyes.

Come to us. Join us. Follow us to form a new society, a new generation where selfies and social media no longer rule the Earth. We are located closer to you than you think. Just follow the midnight signs to your destiny of life-long happiness, free from corruption.

But, beware, any contact with the infected can tempt you to also travel down the same path of self-destruction and death. Avoid the infected at all cost. But, most of all, avoid selfies at all cost. We shall be waiting. Find us at Asylum."

"Holy shit..." Brooke whispers as the small pistol drops from her hand and onto Clare's lifeless body beside her.

"What the fuck am I supposed to do now? The signs. The signs. Where the fuck are the signs?! Why did I even come to this stupid party!? I don't even have a Centriclist! I just came here to get the inside scoop for my blog on the fake lives of influencers!"

Brooke nervously paces throughout the house, the house whose owners may or may never even return. Even if she is to make it out of here alive, the rotting body of Clare continues to follow and haunt her.

"What do I do? What do I do? Do I go? Do I stay? I don't even know where to go! What if that place is a scam? What if it's not even a real place!? Fuck! What do I do!? I've never had to be alone like this before."

Brooke banters back and forth, continuing to pace as she pops open a bottle of rum and chugs away.

Suddenly, she hears a knock on the front door.

"Hello?" The frail voice speaks.

Frightened, Brooke picks up the gun and slowly creeps toward the door. She doesn't know who's still alive during this time, and she's afraid of finding out what lies behind this door.

Maybe it's an actual person. But, maybe, it's also an infected. Maybe it's one of the "consumers." Either way, if it is another human being behind these doors, she needs to find out. She needs to know if she's the sole survivor.

The knocking grows louder as Brooke nears the door, the wooden floors creaking with every step. With one hand lightly touching the doorknob, Brooke slowly turns the knob while the other hand is armed with the pistol.

"Don't move! Hands in the air!" Brooke yells as she finds herself pointing the gun at the young girl she saw earlier through the window, Chloe.

"You! You! I...I...you...you're supposed to be dead! I saw you die!" Brooke stammers, frightened.

"I'll explain later, but right now, you have to come with me! They're coming!" Chloe anxiously gestures.

"Who's 'they'?" Brooke asks, confused.

"No time for questions! Come on! Trust me!" Chloe continues to pressure.

Should I trust her? What if she's lying? What do I really have to lose anyway? Everyone I love is dead.

"I...I need to stop by my mom's first. I need to make sure she's okay," Brooke responds.

"You live on McAdams Street, correct?" Chloe questions suspiciously.

"Yeah...wait! How do you know that?" Brooke interrogates, slightly creeped out that this strange woman from the dead knows so much about her.

"No time for questions! We have to go!" Chloe continues to pull Brooke's arm.

Tired of not knowing what's going on, Brooke holds the gun up to Chloe's head.

"I'm not taking another step until you tell me what the hell is going on here!"

"Whoa, whoa, calm down, Brooke. Put the gun down, and I'll explain."

"Brooke? How do you know my name!?" Brooke walks closer toward Chloe with the gun.

"Please, Brooke, put the gun down. My name is Chloe. Chloe Vandersen. 15 years ago, we were both part of an experiment, an experiment that tested the willpower of the human mind against the influence of social media and the attention of popularity.

Haven't you ever wondered why you always seemed so much less interested in popular social media sites than others, getting into trouble by those around you when you called Centriclist 'stupid'?

We, along with several others, were given an injection known as 'Sys', a serum that turns off the part of our brains that crave instant gratification, and we have been trained to purposefully show up late for social gatherings to avoid the possibility of being exposed to selfies and social media related incidences.

Don't you see!? You and I are the same, the rare few remaining who possess the mutated gene required to stop this virus. When you witnessed me going down earlier, true, the hordes were trying to consume me, trying to get me to become one of them, but the serum automatically sensed the grave danger and blocked out my mental ability to absorb the power of social media and the selfie.

However, a downside to this serum is that, when pressured to the extreme and when forced to acknowledge our own insecurities and flaws, we also risk falling victim to social media and the infection.

Everyone's against the North Koreans because they believe they are the masterminds behind this deadly virus. They're not. The true masterminds are a small group, just a couple hundred miles from here, known as 'Witness', a group that hopes to gain power by eradicating those like us and use our blood to create a new strain that provides humans the ability to resist all temptation, an army of emotionless creatures with the capability of solely focusing on destruction without distraction," Chloe finishes.

"Oh please, this is ridiculous. Do you really expect me to believe all this nonsense? I don't fucking know you! I need to get to my mom!" Brooke interrupts as she tries to push pass Chloe to go outside.

"Brooke! You can't!" Chloe abruptly grabs Brooke's arm and holds her back. "Your...your...mom is dead. I went by your house earlier to find you but, instead, came face-to-face with the midnight matter itself. Your mom is obsessed with Centriclist, correct? I caught her posting a selfie right before 'it' got her. You have to come with me! I know how to keep you safe!"

"D...d...dea...dead?" Brooke stutters as she stumbles backward, tripping on the staircase behind her. "It can't be! You're lying! I'm going to go find my mom, and there is nothing you can do about it. Then, I'm going to Asylum."

"Asylum? You can't! That's what I came here to warn you about! Asylum is where Witness resides. They'll kill you!"

"As opposed to the stalker standing in front of me who won't kill me? I'll take my chances." Brooke proceeds to the door.

"Brooke, NO!" Chloe aggressively pulls Brooke's arm back one more time to prevent her from walking out.

"I warned you, bitch!" With that, Brooke raises the pistol up to Chloe's face once again and pulls the trigger.

To Brooke's surprise, white blood gushes from Chloe's exploding body, turning the ugly carpet of this random house into a crime scene at the North Pole.

What? Brooke wonders. *First, people started expelling black fluids from their bodies, and now white? What next? Green? Blue? The whole freaking rainbow? Was this chick telling the truth? Does she actually have a serum inside her that made her different?*

Does that mean I have white blood too, if blood is even the right word for this enigma? Maybe this virus is worse than anyone had thought. Maybe this white substance is a mutated version of the black substance-induced one.

Whatever it is, I can't take my chances. I need to get to Asylum if I want to survive. But, first, mom's!

Brooke grabs her car keys off the kitchen bar and rushes to her car. She cannot believe the sight she is seeing outside. It is completely bare and empty except for piles upon piles of tiny glass shards covering the sidewalks and roads. It looks like she had just stepped into a smashed jewelry store.

Fumbling with her keys, she finally unlocks the doors and stumbles in to start the ignition.

"Come on, come on. Start! Start, motherfucker!" Brooke curses and bangs on the steering wheel as the engine still refuses to start. "ARGHHHH!! START!!! START!!!"

After several failed attempts, she gets out of the car and pops open the hood…just to find oozes of the black matter coating her entire engine.

"Of course, of course. Just what I needed. FUCK YOU!" Brooke unleashes her pent-up anger as she kicks the front bumper of the car and starts running to her mother's instead, six miles away.

When she finally gets there, exhausted and out of breath, Brooke's heart stops momentarily when she finds her mom's necklace lying on the front lawn, covered in the viral darkness. Her mom loves that necklace and never goes anywhere without it, so when Brooke finds it just lying there, she fears for the worst.

"Mom! Mom! I'm home! Mom! Where are you!?" Brooke shouts as she lets herself into the small modern home and runs in and out of rooms, up and down flights of stairs.

"MOM!!!" She runs over to the kitchen phone and dials her mother's cell. No answer. She tries again. Still no answer. "Pick up, mom. Pick up! Pick up!!"

After sixteen tries, Brooke finally accepts defeat and that Chloe had been right.

It's all my fault. I should have warned her. I should never have taught her how to use Centriclist or even a camera. I exposed her to this disgusting and cruel world. If I had just kept her naïve, I would still have her in my life.

A single tear trickles down Brooke's cheek as she drops to her knees and into a pile of her own mother.

Scooping up a small sample of the substance from her mother's remains, she places it into the miniature gold locket around her neck.

IN SEARCH FOR TRUTH

"We're here in New York City, and a mysterious virus is spreading at an exponential rate. Person after person is liquefying into some strange black material and shattering into thin air as Centriclist posts are on the rise."

"Signs. I need signs," Brooke stammers to herself as she tries to look out for signs that will take her to Asylum, hopefully, in one piece.

"Asylum! Give me a sign!" She shouts out into the sky.

Great. How the fuck am I supposed to get to this place if I have no idea what or who I'm looking for, with no one to ask in this deserted ghost town?

Brooke continues walking several miles north, her feet giving out with each painful step.

"A sign. A sign. I need a sign. That's it, I'm going to die here."

Suddenly, Brooke encounters another odd phenomenon. Her locket begins to vibrate, as if some small demon is trying to make its way out. She looks down at her chest and sees her gold locket bouncing up and down, possessed.

As she tries to hold the locket down, the thin gold chain pulls against her neck and puts her in a chokehold, suppressing her ability to breathe.

Seconds later, the chain rips off her neck and falls onto the patch of grass in front of her. As Brooke leans closer toward it to pick it up, what looks like black blood begins leaking out of the small cracks of the locket, spilling all over the ground.

Dipping her right index finger into the black substance, she realizes that this is the same black substance that has been engulfing millions of people around the world. She looks down at the ground again and notices that the material is beginning to form a message, perhaps a word or a symbol.

"Follow the road less traveled by. Embark on a journey to the destination rarely seen. Go where no one else has desired to go."

Where no one else has desired to go? Destination rarely seen? What does that mean? Brooke contemplates as a scream is suddenly heard from a distance, a cry so faint yet seems so close.

Brooke races over to that direction and sees a young man, maybe five years younger than her, running toward her direction.

"Get out of the way! Run for your life! Save yourself!" The man screams to Brooke as he continues running.

What? "What's going on?" Brooke asks, confused.

"No time to explain! Just run!"

Brooke looks behind the man and sees a crowd of what used to be human beings, chasing after him with their smartphones, their faces and bodies all covered with the same black matter that has been affecting everyone in town.

"NO! NO! NO!" The man screams in agony as the crowd catches up to him and surrounds him, with clicks and flashes heard in the process, the same incidence she had experienced with Chloe.

Is this man the same kind as Chloe? Could he possibly give me some answers?

"Excuse me, sir! Let me help you! Sir? I have a couple of questions I think you can answer for me," Brooke questions the man, unsure of whether to help or not.

"Just run! Run before they get you too!" The man continues to shriek until his voice is suppressed by the horde surrounding him.

Brooke can visibly see splatters of blood shoot up into the air. Hoping this man is like Chloe and that he isn't actually gone forever, she stands there and waits for him to come through the crowd, fist up like a warrior.

Instead, she is met with asphalt covered in black liquid and a small pile of glass shards as the horde turns around and heads toward her way, fast!

"Shit..." Brooke whispers quietly, backing away before transforming into a full-fire sprint, away from the crowd.

Shit. Shit. Shit. Brooke thinks as she continues to run, her feet tearing apart as her 4-inch boots begin to rip into her.

Crap. They're catching up. I need to lose them before they tear into me too! I refuse to become one of them. Wait...haha...become one of them? I'll be dead before that happens.

Brooke continues to deliberate as she makes a sharp turn into the barren forest. Weeds and cacti pierce into her as she tries to lose herself amongst the trees, enough to avoid the mob.

Continuing to run, she sees a small cave with the corner of her eye and bolts toward it to hide. Pulling a tree branch over her face, she prays that the infected are stupid enough to bypass her without noticing, and with her luck, they do...all except for one...one young once-makeup influencer on Centriclist now turned confused and unstable. She sniffs around, Brooke fearing that this "thing" can actually smell her out. She does.

The influencer slowly creeps her way toward Brooke's location, continuing to sniff, until she suddenly stiffens and cracks, shattering moments later.

Shit. That was close. What the hell is going on with this world? It's like everyone's fucking possessed or something and can't seem to break out of it.

"Wait, what did that thing, or whatever it was, say? 'Go where no one else has desired to go.' Where no one else has desired to go? What the hell does that mean? Okay, focus, Brooke. Let's see. We know that this virus spreads when people take selfies and become super obsessed with Centriclist and social media."

"So...this has to have something to do with selfies." Brooke continues. "Selfies...where no one has the desire to go...selfies...places people don't want to go. What ruins selfies? How do people take selfies? Think, Brooke, think! Damn it, this is one of those times I wish I had used social media!

What does Kayla always say when she takes pictures? 'I hate the way my ass looks. I wish my boobs are bigger. My lips are lopsided.' I got it! The place where no one else has desired to go is the place that shows the true reflections of people.

The Museum of Mirrors! I got it! I got it!" Brooke cheers while jumping up and down until she realizes there's no one around to celebrate with her, foolishly standing there alone.

BROOKE'S TEMPTATION

"Shit, I'm walking in the wrong direction," Brooke curses to herself as she realizes she had walked 30 miles north of town when she was supposed to head south.

While turning around, she walks past several more selfie-taking obsessed victims, lying in strange poses in the middle of streets and completely unaware of the others liquefying beside them until it becomes too late, and they liquefy themselves.

Why are people so stupid and ignorant?

"LOOK AROUND YOU, PEOPLE! STOP TAKING DAMN SELFIES UNLESS YOU WANT TO FUCKING DIE!"

Unfortunately, no one hears her, all either consumed in their own self-absorbed habits or in the process of being consumed by the virus.

What has this world become?

As Brooke continues to walk, she hears a meek cry to her right. She turns her head and sees a woman, roughly her age, sitting on the steps of a dilapidated house. Curious and guilty if she doesn't stop to help, Brooke approaches her.

"Hey, are you okay?" Brooke asks.

"No...this stupid virus. It's killing everyone I love! And I can't do anything to stop it. I told them not to use Centriclist, but they continue to do so anyway! Now, I'm all alone and forced to watch everyone I love around me die!" The woman continues to cry.

"I know how you feel. I was at a party and watched all my friends die right before my eyes. It's horrifying. No one knows what this is. No one can stop it. What's your name?" Brooke questions the woman in an attempt to use small talk to console her.

"Dani," the woman answers.

"Dani, I think I know how to get help, or at least get to a place of sanctuary. There's this place called 'Asylum' that is supposed to keep us safe from the virus. I think I know where it is. You should come with me."

"Asylum? Is this a joke? We're all doomed. There is no hope for us!"

"Trust me! I'm heading there right now. It's a whole lot better than sitting here, hating life and wishing your loved ones come back. Come on, follow me."

Dani reluctantly agrees and gets up from the steps to follow Brooke. They continue walking for several more miles, talking to each other about their childhoods, their friends, their families, their lives before this pandemic, and Dani is surprised to find out that Brooke also hates the idea of social media and the Internet.

"Wow! I've never met anyone else who doesn't have a Centriclist account. I thought I was the only one! That's so cool!" Dani exclaims.

"Hey, Dani, I have a question for you. Have you ever heard of a serum that…?" Brooke begins to speak when she suddenly gets interrupted.

"Oh my god! Brooke! Look as this beautiful sunset! It's absolutely PERFECT against these mountains! Come on, we have to take a picture together to remember this special moment! #survivors," Dani exclaims, leaving Brooke confused.

"Picture?" Brooke questions suspiciously.

Just before Dani snaps the photo, Brooke pushes her aside and backs away.

"You said you hate selfies. You said you don't take them. What the hell is this? Why did you lie to me?" Brooke demands as she continues to back away.

"Awww, come on, Brooke, just one little selfie. It won't kill you," Dani persists, closing in on Brooke.

"No! No! I don't want it! I don't want the virus! Stay away!"

"Come join us, Brooke. You know you want to. It will be the best experience of your life. Centriclist is life!" Dani speaks, eerily and almost possessed.

The black matter begins leaking out of her eyes, and she looks like something out of a torture movie.

Continuing to back away, Brooke stumbles and falls, her lower waist colliding against a hard-angular surface. She feels behind her and realizes that she had taken the gun with her after shooting Chloe. Pulling it out, she points it at Dani.

"Don't come any closer, or I'll shoot!"

However, what Brooke fails to remember is that nothing distracts the selfie-obsessed. Nothing deters the virus from its main target: to possess. Brooke shoots several times, just to realize her bullets are going straight through Dani as if she's made of liquid.

"Fuck!" Brooke curses as she throws the gun at Dani, which becomes absorbed in her body.

"Stay back!" She screams as she gets up and continues to run.

Why isn't she shattering?! She's supposed to die by now!

Brooke eventually reaches the museum and goes inside. Dani follows in close behind but immediately shatters as she comes face-to-face with her own reflection. Squinting her eyes as she witnesses Dani shatter before her, Brooke explores the museum.

Every inch of its interior is covered with mirrors, enhancing every flaw of every reflection. She has never seen anything like it. She walks up the stairs and finds something written in blood on the largest mirror in the building, "Welcome to Your Demise."

Demise? What is this? What demise?

"Hello!? Hello?! Is anyone here?" Brooke shouts out.

No answer.

"Hello!?" Brooke shouts out again.

Still no answer.

While exploring the building trying to look for someone, anyone, Brooke suddenly stops in front of an intriguing mirror, a mirror that seems to call to her. For some reason, she cannot take her eyes off it.

"It's magnificent."

However, the mirror takes a dark turn and begins amplifying all the flaws and blemishes that Brooke has, her pores, her stomach rolls, her cellulite, her grey hairs, her acne scars, the list goes on and on.

"Who the hell am I?! Why am I so ugly?!" She cries out, fingernails tearing at her eyelids until they start to bleed. Brooke falls to the ground and begins pinching the rolls on her thighs and pulling at the skin on her neck. "I hate my body! I hate the way my disgusting body looks! Why do I look like this!?"

Brooke never had an issue with her body before. In fact, she never really cared that much about how she appeared to others; however, until now. It is as if these mirrors' amplification of her skyrocketed and possessed her insecurity, and now, all she seems to care about is her external appearance.

She cannot take her eyes off the thousands of mirrors in front of her, picking at every flaw on her body and cursing herself for existing.

Suddenly, more words begin to appear on the mirrors:

"Do you wish to change?"

"Do I wish to change? Hell yeah! I want to change my fucking body! I hate myself so much that I can't stop examining every ounce of ugliness."

"If you wish to change, please take a selfie of yourself, and you will become the most beautiful person on Earth. You will have no more flaws or imperfections. You will be PERFECT!"

"But, I can't!" Brooke stammers. "I can't take a selfie of myself because of the virus! I'll die! But, then again, I'm so ugly and disgusting that I'd rather die than continue living like this. I can't live with myself like this. Since I'm going to die anyway, what do I really have to lose?"

Brooke fumbles through her pockets to find her phone. *I know I grabbed it. I know I have it on me.*

"Aha! I got it! Shit! 5% left!?"

With her battery dying, Brooke turns on her camera, and with her hands shaking, she flips the camera around to selfie mode. Flashing a fake smile to show off her good side, Brooke takes her selfie.

Suddenly, something overtakes her. Her one single selfie suddenly becomes hundreds as Brooke feels a sensation surpass her, electricity shivering down her spine. Her eyes widen like an unrealistic doll-like face, and her hands tremble, pushing her phone closer and closer to her face.

Suddenly, she becomes obsessed. She becomes hungry, craving selfies and Centriclist fame as her sole sources of energy.

"I need selfies. I need selfies now!" Brooke gratingly repeats to herself over and over as she rushes to download the Centriclist app, creating an account under the name @borderlinebrooke and posting her selfie with #thebitchhasarrived.

Within minutes, her account receives over 500 likes and 200 followers. That set her off.

Brooke becomes addicted.

Over the next several days, Brooke continues to take and post selfies on her Centriclist page, completely oblivious to those around her who continue to liquefy and shatter.

She has taken up the social personality of a punk-rock fashion queen, looting clothing stores that have gone out of business when the owners shattered from the deadly virus.

Since she knows she isn't getting caught, as almost half of the town's population have disappeared, why not just make the best out of the situation and score some free clothes in the process?

Her first stop in her new quest is the most popular and exclusive punk clothing store within 50 miles of town named, "Shit Rock," known for its chain-adorned leather jackets and silver spiked shoes, favorites among all celebrities and influencers but comes at a high cost of $2,000 per item.

Feeling her newfound freedom to take whatever she wants without consequences and the high need to impress, Brooke chooses a lime-green ruffle chiffon knee-length dress, glitter black spiked and chain pumps, and a safety pin inspired statement necklace, strips down to her bare skin in the middle of the store with no shame, and throws on her new clothes.

Several moments before she entered the store, Brooke smashed all the mirrors with her fists as they would be detrimental to her Centriclist life. She cannot stand the chance of having her real body image exposed to herself or to anyone else. The only image she is allowed is the one she decides she wants to show.

However, since Brooke entered the world of selfies and social media too late in the game, just when all the social media goers are beginning to perish from the world, Brooke is left with less potential followers and likes than she would have gotten if she had joined months before, leaving her unsatisfied with her low counts, despite her large efforts to alter her photos into the best they can be.

Because she now needs to feel validated for her amazing selfies, something she never cared about before, she begins engaging in drastic measures, buying fake bot followers and creating hundreds of accounts on her own to make them seem like they are unique people with unique accounts when, in reality, it is one person with thousands of fake accounts.

She uses these fake accounts she creates to interact with her main account, making herself seem more popular and liked than she actually is.

THE DOWNFALL OF WITNESS

"Where the hell is she!? She should be here by now! I thought I told you to entice Brooke Harfield to come to Asylum! We need her to complete our quest of eradicating social media and human opinions forever! Everyone else succeeded in rounding up the others injected with Sys. Where the hell is your bait?!"

The leader of Witness, Jacques, grabs his associate, Sylvester, by the collar of his shirt, his feet lifting off the ground, and throws him across the room, smashing into a box filled with binders upon binders labeled: "Brooke Harfield."

Witness has been following and documenting the lives of children injected with Sys for decades, waiting for this very moment. They are the deadly masterminds behind this mind-inflicting virus, blaming the North Koreans and using them as scapegoats so they can step in as "heroes" at just the right time and get the Sys members to trust them, trust them enough to sacrifice their lives to them.

They are sick of people having opinions, sick of people online pretending to be Internet personalities and social media influencers, sick of people bragging about lives that do not actually exist, and sick of people pretending to be unique and special when they do the same things that everyone else does.

Jacques used to have a social media account, a decent 50,000 followers on Centriclist while promoting his new clothing line, "Vox."

However, with the typical social media world, his account soon fell victim to online bullying and trolling from those who had "higher influences" than him for reasons completely superficial. Jacques felt bullied off social media, and he never looked back, spending his entire life plotting against destroying Centriclist and their bullshit opinions.

"Bring me Brooke NOW! Or you'll be replacing her." Jacques throws Sylvester across the room once again, nearing him with a sharp knife before severing off his pinky as a warning, sending Sylvester into a frenzy of screams and agony.

Meanwhile...

"Hey, Centrabitches! Guess who's drinking a super skinny vanilla latte!!? OMG, I can't wait to go shopping later and buy this adorable leather pair of pumps I've been eyeing for months! It's uber expensive, but who cares, I can afford it because I'm effin' awesome! See ya later, babes!" Brooke speaks into her smartphone as she posts a video to her many Centriclist stories before handing the cup of water back to the kid she stole it from.

While walking to Sassa Mall to buy, or rather pilfer, a pair of shoes she would never wear but has decided it would make the perfect post, she feels a tranquilizer dart suddenly pierce the back of her neck as she drops and shatters her phone. Lying there in broad daylight, people continue to walk right past her as they remain too preoccupied with their own social media lives to notice an unconscious girl lying in the middle of the road.

Hours later, Brooke wakes up and finds herself locked in a metal cage in the pitch of darkness.

"What the fuck?!" Brooke panics as she looks around her. "Where the fuck am I!?"

She runs over to the barred door and tugs on it. "Where the hell am I? Let me out! Let me out!"

"You can save your breath, honey. None of us are getting out." Brooke hears a sassy man yell back at her.

"What? Who's there?"

"It doesn't matter, honey bear. We'll all be done for in a few minutes anyway," the voice speaks out again.

"Oh, Christoph, stop messing with her." Brooke hears a different voice, a woman this time, call out. "You're at Asylum, girl. You know, that voice announcing safety from the virus that seems too good to be true? Well, it fucking is! And now they gonna kill us."

"Asylum? Chloe was right?" Brooke whispers quietly to herself but loud enough for the others to hear her.

"Wait, hold up a minute!" The woman screams out. "You know Chloe? How you know Chloe?"

"She...she...uh...came to visit me a few days ago. I thought I saw her die, but then she came knocking on my front door. She tried to warn me about Asylum and some group named 'Witness', and told me not to go, but I refused to listen," Brooke responds nervously, fearful of where this conversation is heading.

"Where's Chloe now, honey bear? She escaped from Asylum about a week ago to try to warn the other Sys members about Witness. Witness needs only six of us to complete their little experiment. Chloe wanted to make sure the rest stayed away because without six of us, they would continue holding off on killing us until they found the last person. Clearly, Chloe either threw us all under the bus, or you're incredibly stupid." Christoph's blunt honesty begins to really strike Brooke's conscience.

"She...uh...she...I...," Brooke stutters, wanting to avoid telling the truth but knowing that would make matters worse.

"Spit it out, woman!" A deeper voice from further away exclaims.

"I killed her!" Brooke confesses, guilt overwhelming her as she utters each word. "I didn't believe her because what she was saying seemed too out of the ordinary to be true, so I shot her because she didn't move out of my way."

"Too out of the ordinary!? Like a virus turning everyone into black sludge and causing them to shatter into glass shards is completely normal??!" Christoph shouts, anger fuming out of him with his head about to explode.

"I didn't know..." Brooke begins as the lights all turn on, and the sound of drums begin to beat.

"Captives! Captives! It is time for the ceremony to begin!" A voice announces, sending echoes throughout the building.

One by one, the side door of each cell cracks open, exposing the captives to a stadium of a cheering audience as Brooke comes in contact with each of the other five, all of whom are chained to metal poles.

"Ladies and gentlemen! This is the moment you have all been waiting for. The moment where social media shall no longer exist, and people will no longer have their own stubborn opinions of the world. No longer will we have demonstrators. No longer will we have social justice warriors. No longer will we have these so-called fake influencers ruling the world like it's their own.

Today is the day of redemption! Today is the day temptation and social pressure no longer exist! Today, we eradicate Centriclist FOREVER!" Jacques, dressed in a velvet purple tailcoat announces into his microphone as the audience cheers with every sentence.

Brooke cannot believe how many people are actually against social media. The entire stadium is full of people cheering for her to die just so the world will no longer have influencers. She looks over at the other captives, all of whom are staring toward the center of the stadium, both frightened and in awe. Brooke glances over and sees a giant fire pit surrounded by six electrocution chairs, all hooked to needles and tubes.

That's it. This is how I die. This is how I die because of my damn stupidity. Brooke thinks to herself.

"For those of you unfamiliar with the process, these six Sys members, or 'Systics' as I like to call them, have a special serum inside of them that allows their minds to resist the powers of social temptation, leaving them invincible to the deadly virus currently plaguing the Earth.

The only reason this virus is able to destroy the human population as much as it has is because the human population have become brainwashed by the temptations of society: Centriclist followers, selfies, filters, fame, and clout.

Fear no more! With the scarlet embers of these six Systics, I will create a new virus, a new virus that prevents the human mind from succumbing to these deadly temptations of society, a virus where social pressure can no longer affect us, allowing us to remain powerful and undefeatable.

Now, let's begin phase one of my genius plan! Guards, strap these captives down please!" The audience cheers louder as several burly men behind Jacques unchain Brooke and the other captives from their poles and drag them over to the chairs, strapping them in one by one.

"Now, we will begin the exsanguination process, draining each and every one of these Systics of their very essence," Jacques continues, smiling to himself in pride.

Brooke wishes she could scream, bite, escape, whatever it will take to get away from this torture hell. However, her mouth has been gagged and taped, and her body has been restrained from all movement as over thirty needles are pierced into her veins.

She watches in horror as bodies of the other captives drain to nothingness, faces pale, lives gone.

"Hahahaha, soon the world shall be free!!!" Jacques exclaims in joy before he becomes disappointingly interrupted.

"Uh...sir? We have a problem." One of his men calls out to him, gesturing to the large test tube over the fire where the supposedly and expected red blood has suddenly turned a deep purple.

"What the hell is this?" Jacques becomes furious, fully knowing why his plan had been tarnished. He turns to the captives, his face infuriated with different shades of red, "Who the FUCK is INFECTED?!"

He turns to his men, "Which one of you brought me an infected captive!?"

His men continue to stare back and forth at each other, unsure of whether to speak.

"Which one of you brought me an INFECTED?!" Jacques screams again.

Before he has the chance to take further actions, the vial over the fire pit begins to shake, rumbling the entire stadium. The audience screams as the vial becomes more and more unstable, smoke and steam shooting out the top as the liquid concoction bubbles and fizzes.

"Everybody leave, NOW! Everyone, get the fuck out!" Jacques announces to the audience, unsure of the consequences of mixing infected blood with Sys blood.

The audience runs and pushes each other to the ground, attempting to escape the stadium. Jacques guns down his men, one by one, as his anger for his fouled plan overwhelms him.

He remains frozen in the middle of the stadium, unsure of what to do next, as the vial finally explodes and the substance evaporates into the air, glass shattering and shooting at each and every person within a 2-mile radius of the stadium, including Jacques himself.

...

Since the explosion, in combination with the rapid effects of the virus, towns and cities all over the world have become more and more deserted, with famously large cities like New York City, Hong Kong, and Paris reducing to a mere five residents per county, if even.

Businesses are being looted and boarded up as they have gone out of business. Animal shelters are rotting with carcasses as there is no one left in these towns to feed the canines and felines or release them from their cages. Strays and the homeless are left eating each other as there are no other sources of food or water. The world is becoming darker and darker, crumbling to the virus that has taken over the human mind.

Suddenly, we see a strange phenomenon. The smartphones left behind by those who have shattered into dust begin to tremble, on the streets, in homes, and on the seats of cars. A ray of light shoots out from the screens of these phones and radiates into the sky, illuminating regions and blinding those who still exist.

This beam of light lasts for approximately 13 minutes before it suddenly disappears, and in its place are, surprisingly, hundreds of thousands of newly-reincarnated "people."

Where did all these people come from? Wasn't everyone consumed and destroyed by the virus? Now, the Earth is adorned with a new generation walking its face.

However, these are not just ordinary people. These so-called "people" are the bots and fake accounts that hopeful social media influencers have bought and created, respectively, over the years to enhance the success of their accounts, now rising into three dimensional beings since the infusion of the Systics and the infected.

The only interaction these bots and falsified beings can have is the ability to swipe away those they do not like, sending them to shatter themselves, and the ability to swipe toward them those they want as followers, creating a magnetic effect that pulls in the few real people left on Earth and forcing them to fully engage in the accounts of these bots and falsified creatures.

The only words these bots and fake beings can speak are "clout," "influencer," "selfie," and "hashtag," never being able to form full conversations in person but has the ability to create online presences that resemble those of actual users.

A NEW GENERATION

Generations later, we see a new world, a world where Centriclist has taken over. People no longer have jobs, hobbies, or responsibilities. Their sole focus in life has become Centriclist. They live and breathe Centriclist, taking selfies like it's their only purpose in life.

The sole purpose of this new lifestyle is to either gain or maintain followers. Those who lose even one follower immediately shatter from the face of the Earth as their existences will have become worthless. Life has become a competition, survival of the most popular selfies. Those who do not measure up are wiped from society as if they had never been born.

Years ago, the world had been destroyed, people vanished from the virus that plagued everyone's minds. Country after country saw drastic losses in their citizens, with nothing they could have done to prevent this annihilation.

Those who did survive, the very few who were not infected by the virus, either hid in isolation or committed suicide due to the horrors they had witnessed around them. Soon, there are only ten remaining, six women and four men, on the planet who endured the apocalypse.

However, these few survivors do not know that they are the only ones left. In fact, they believe that everyone walking amongst them are all survivors.

But, other than those six women and four men, this new generation, this new generation of "civilians" walking amongst them are all bots and fabricated people created by those of the previous generation, those who had risen from the smartphones of the deceased when the blood of the infected had mixed in with the blood of the Systics.

Because the wrath of the virus still exists, living in this new world comes with many rules, with those breaking the rules splintering to their deaths.

All citizens must rise at 4am every morning, no exceptions, and prepare themselves for their first selfie of the day: the early morning bed head (without the actual bed head, of course).

They must then prepare themselves to take a selfie of the best sunrise moment they can capture, all while taking a selfie with the most beautiful breakfast just a few short hours later.

Each person has been assigned an Internet personality to follow, ranging from travel blogger to foodie to fitness influencer to health nut to fashion guru. They must adhere to these personalities and live by them even if they despise who they are.

Each Internet personality must take at least 20 selfies a day of their daily lives, showcase them with the perfect filters, and post them at the designated times. Everyone must strive to do whatever they can to avoid annihilation.

If any of the ten survivors are to rebel, they would immediately turn into a bot, forced to roam the planet on a programmed brain forever. All around the world, bot after bot are roaming the Earth on their phones.

They seem eerily like real people, but they are incapable of pulling away from their phones and incapable of engaging in any other conversation besides those related to selfies and Centriclist.

Despite being bots, these "people" behave as ordinary people, capable of engaging with social media content and unfollowing those they please.

A few blocks away from the crippling world of bots in Arsanville, Katria wakes up in her luxury and modern condo, 56 stories in the air. Katria is one of the few remaining people, or "nomalies," as they are referred. Before the virus wiped out her former world, Katria hated social media.

She never had a Centriclist account and always mocked those taking selfies, disgusted by self-absorbed hacks trying to be people they're not and ruining vacations for everyone else.

She had a best friend, Kayla, who was always obsessed with social media. Sure, she didn't have the prettiest face in the world, but the Internet never found out anyway as she always covered up her true appearance with filters and alterations.

Her picture-perfect model exterior did not match who she really was. But she didn't give two shits about living a life of honesty. She kept receiving attention, mostly from men, so she continued, always taking pictures of herself wherever she went and never putting down her phone for more than 10 minutes.

Katria had been hiding in the bomb shelter of one of her neighbors when she heard that the spread of the virus was killing everyone, with no phone and no contact with anyone else in the outside world. She had been in isolation for over six years until she woke up one day wearing a white-colored ball gown and lying on a bed of flowers, her mind completely wiped of the deadly incident and full of memories she could not remember as truths.

"Rise and shine, my fellow Centrics!" Katria speaks into her video camera as she live streams her morning rise on Centriclist, her model-thin body dressed in white laced panties and a white satin babydoll that barely hangs over her waist.

She curls up in her soft white comforter, midnight black waves dangling over her shoulders. Katria is designated as a beauty makeup model, her social media posts and images centered around her flawless skin and perfect facial features. She has over 2 million followers on Centriclist, and her account continues to grow every day as she posts provocative images of herself in various locations: on her bed, by her pool, at a café, and even in her bath tub.

"So, today I have a full day planned out for us," Katria continues to stream. "After my shower, I'm going to test out my new makeup collection from Marcy Kaye that LITERALLY just came in the mail last night, and I am super obsessed with their products, like super! Don't worry, guys. I'll keep you all in the loop when I test these out.

Next, I'm going to fix myself a green smoothie with kale, avocado, spinach, and soy milk to get me through the morning as I head off to my photoshoot at L'Saunt, a super exclusive modeling agency that only hires the very best.

Like, seriously, guys. Models from L'Saunt get booked for gigs on major fashion magazines like VG and Xan't. Eek!! I'm so, so excited! Alright, babes, check back with you soon! Kat peacing out!"

Shortly after ending her live stream, Katria places her phone on her tripod, turns on her lamps to brighten up the room, and spreads out across her bed, lingerie risen up to her waist and legs crossed over each other. She then blows a kiss toward the camera as the countdown finishes, and the phone camera snaps.

"Hmm...what filter should I use today? How about 'Babe by the Beach'? Everyone loves a great beach look!"

Katria speaks softly to herself as she throws on #morningsrock and posts her selfie before stepping into the shower.

"Hey, babes! Kat's back! So, as I promised, I'm going to test out my new collection of Marcy Kaye products for you all!" Katria speaks excitedly as she goes back onto her live stream after her shower.

Only wearing a towel, she continues to speak into the camera. "For all of you who are always asking about my makeup routine, here it is! First, I take this bare skin all-natural foundation, after washing my face, of course, and polish my face, making sure to cover every section and every blemish. Then, I take my eyebrow pencil and lightly brush my brows to make them fuller.

Next, I take this black eyeliner and carefully line my eyes, followed by a midnight eyeshadow to slowly brush over my lids, pressing my eyes together to really give it that smoky effect. Finally, after curling my lashes, I take this extra luminous volume mascara and gently brush my lashes to make my eyes pop. I throw on some gloss, run a brush through my hair, and voila, my perfect look!

Alright, babes, that's all for today. Tune in tomorrow as I demonstrate my routine to show you how to look like a mystical fairy!"

Placing her phone on her tripod once again after stopping her live stream, Katria poses for her selfie, uses an app to remove the excess skin from her face and shape her head to form a heart, and posts her final result with #allnaturale.

"Well, that's enough of that. Perfect! Shit, I'm late for my photoshoot!" Katria yells out as she looks over at the clock and realizes that her makeup routine had taken longer than she had expected.

Grabbing her purse and rushing out the door, but not forgetting to take a #lateforshoot selfie first, Katria bolts out her front door and into the streets. The streets in her town, and other towns as well, aren't like what they once were.

Before the apocalypse, people seemed more genuine, mostly miserable and stressed, but genuine. There was purpose and a story behind people's smiles, and only a handful of the countries had fake personalities who tried to make something of themselves online.

Now, however, the streets are completely filled with aspiring Internet stars, bots who strive to become influencers, and a society where the sole focus is Internet fame and popularity.

Walking the streets, the civilians must always be on social media, even when crossing the intersections and driving. Everyone moves with robotic steps, always alert for paparazzi trying to take pictures of their celebrity statuses.

Whenever they aren't monotonously walking with their heads buried into their phones, they are posing, posing for selfies whenever they see the chance, ranging from dangling off bridges to standing on top of moving trains to documenting everything they put into their mouths, sometimes things that aren't even edible.

The world has become a different world, a strange world fixated on cyber personalities.

SECOND STRAIN

"That's it, Katria. Work it! Work it, girl!" Knoz, the photographer at L'Sant calls out as Katria poses for the camera in Ysekes' new clothing line. "Ooh, show me that face. Gorgeous! Pucker those lips. Fantastic!"

Knoz continues as he snaps his camera, turning his camera around several times to snap images of himself.

As a photographer on Centriclist, Knoz is actually a fake account created by Brooke during her maniacal obsession with social media, a stereotypical homosexual male who prides himself on his slick man buns, chiseled jaw, polished cuticles, and floral neckerchiefs.

He uses pity to gain the attention of new followers with his fabricated life story of being a victim of bullying as a child for wanting to be expressive and creative.

He pretty much had to raise himself growing up as his father would always beat him for not dressing "normal," and his mother would always side with his father, fearful of getting beat herself.

Because of that, Knoz swore to himself that he would never change his personality for anyone or for any reason, flaunting his flawless makeup and stylish fashion style like it's nobody's business.

"Work it! Hmm, girl. You look so amazing, like I'm so jealous. I just love your flawless skin! How you doin' that, girl?" Knoz playfully questions Katria.

"Oh, Knoz, you and I both know that we can never tell. Queens are queens because queens keep secrets!"

"Speaking of secrets, a little birdie told me a little special someone is going to be the new cover model for VG," Knoz whispers as he places his index finger over his glossy lips in silence.

"REALLY?!? Oh my god!! Knoz, you're the freaking best! I love you!! Come on, babe, this calls for a selfie. Squeeze in, and smile!"

"No, wait, girl, I gotta fix my bun!" Knoz fusses as Katria snaps the camera.

Dissatisfied with the image she sees on her camera, Katria, as usual, decides to polish up her selfie before posting it onto the Internet, using photo apps that can re-shape her face and help her drop pounds instantly.

However, seconds after posting her altered selfie, where she had shrunken her nose and removed the wrinkles from her forehead, Katria feels a strange sensation. Her eyes begin to blur, and her head begins to spin. Ignoring her symptoms, she takes a look at the selfie she had just taken and admires her picture-perfect appearance.

"Knoz, excuse me one second, I feel a little light-headed; I need to go freshen up."

"Mmm hmm, you do you." Knoz waves Katria off as he becomes fixated on posting his own selfie onto his social media account.

"Come on, Kat, get it together! Get it together!" Katria repeats to herself as she closes the bathroom door behind her and splashes her face with cold water.

"Get it together! Get it to..."

Suddenly, Katria freezes as she notices something strange in the mirror. Her nose has suddenly become larger, and the wrinkles on her forehead have become more prominent than usual, exact opposites of what Katria had done to her photo, a realization she fails to piece together.

"No, no, no!" Katria continues to repeat as she takes out her concealer in attempts to hide her wrinkles. She then tears off the bottom half of her peasant skirt to cover up her nose.

No way can she let Knoz see her like this; he'll take VG away from her for sure. No, she has to remain disguised until she can find a way to fix this mess.

"Kat, my darling, you okay in there?" Katria hears Knoz knocking on the door.

Still paralyzed from what she saw in the mirror, Katria finishes tying the piece of fabric around her face before bolting out the door.

"Knoz, I need to go. I...uh...have a family emergency and need to leave. Let's reschedule!"

Katria runs past Knoz and into a dark alleyway where she can be sure no one can see her. She passes more brainwashed citizens walking in monotonous steps, eyes glued to their phones, as she pulls out her own phone in the alley and snaps another selfie.

To her surprise, her face looks even uglier. Her nose has become even larger, her forehead wrinklier, and no amount of makeup is enough to cover up her monstrous face, despite how good of an artist she is.

Ding! Ding! Ding!

Katria's alarm goes off as she realizes it's time to post another selfie. She attempts to take the best one she can under unfortunate circumstances, uses an app to enhance the size of her breasts and shrink the size of her waist, slaps on a bright filter, and sends it off...just before her breasts flatten, and her stomach bloats.

SOCIAL MEDIA'S NEW NORMAL

Small, pale heads peek out from behind curtains of darkened buildings. Their eyes are far too large for their faces, and crooked yellow teeth stand prominent against the day's dying light.

Nearly nine months have passed since the new generation discovered that photo filters have become the demise of society, turning people into the very parts of themselves they strive so hard to avoid, yet, the side effects of self-obsession and vain still linger amongst the societies.

Phones remain glued to petite-sized hands, social media influencers have become uglier and uglier, just as their feeds are becoming more and more glamourous with more and more followers. Yet, they do not stop.

Despite their physical appearances becoming more like burn victims, society continues to alter their selfies and images in attempts to show the world they are worth paying attention to. They cannot bear to lose any followers and risk becoming extinct; they must do everything they can to keep going, at all costs.

However, by now, society has forgotten about the virus, the virus that had tormented the world for living in vain. This social media obsessed society has become so fixated on taking the perfect selfie and avoiding social media exile that memories of the deadly obsessed virus had disappeared.

The virus had been non-prevalent for years now, and this new generation now creates a novel world that would have been shunned by the last.

Remi and his younger sister, Iris, are two of the remaining survivors who had been in hiding during the apocalypse. They lie, dressed in clean white robes, on a circular marble table beneath a bright chandelier, trapped in some sort of chamber with needles and IV tubes pierced into their veins.

They remain motionless, almost as if they aren't even alive. The room remains quiet, still, as if no one else is in the building with them. They lie, asleep, peaceful, in dreams. Suddenly, a stream of blood begins to trickle out of the corner of Remi's eye.

"Axel, it's happening again. Please inject the boy on the left with 100mg of likasitol," A voice from the overhead speakers announce.

A strange man dressed completely in black arises from out of nowhere with a large needle and towers over Remi. He grabs Remi's right arm and begins to inject the substance, not realizing that Remi's eyes are beginning to twitch.

"What the hell is happening to me!?" Remi springs up from the table, causing the needle to scrape against his forearm, as he attempts to pull away from Axel and free himself from the tubes.

He manages to kick Axel in the shin before pushing him onto the ground and running over to his sister.

"Iris, wake up! You have to wake up!"

However, distracted with trying to wake his sister up, Remi fails to see a metal chair whack across the back of his head as he goes back down onto the ground, lying still once again, this time, his blood darkening.

...

A week after the incident that Remi has no recollection of, he watches his sister, Iris, snap a picture of herself in their apartment kitchen, unaware of anything that had happened to her besides her booming social media following. She flashes a sweet and innocent smile for her phone's camera, one hand pushing back her brunette locks as she attempts to capture the best image she possibly can.

Iris is a yogi influencer on Centriclist, so her body must always be flawless and fit. However, she notices a small flab of skin beneath her chin and brushes over it with a filter to remove it before posting. Shortly after posting, she feels her neck enhancing, enlarging as she finds it more difficult to swallow, a terrifying side effect for those who feel the need to alter their images.

"Jesus, Iris, can't you just post your selfies as is for once?" Remi asks as he notices Iris's enlarged neck.

"Oh, Remi, you of all people should know that I can't. If I post even one flaw, I risk dying. It's not a move I'm willing to attempt," Iris responds, fearfully, as she accepts her swollen neck. "Besides, I'm probably just allergic to something I ate. It's no big deal."

This dangerous side effect rose shortly after the world of social media had boomed, and social hopefuls trying to rise to the top have become more and more insecure about their natural appearances not measuring up to the standards for receiving followers.

Losing confidence and fearing the risk of death, the rate of people using photo apps to enhance their images has skyrocketed to the point where Centriclist had malfunctioned and began instigating in users the exact opposite of portraits of the people they are trying to conceive.

Even children are spending money they do not have to buy whatever app or filter they can to enhance their profiles and keep their spirits alive. They want to look good for the Internet. They need to please all those around them and avoid losing followers. It no longer matters what people look like in reality, as long as their social feeds appear as perfect.

People in towns begin smashing mirrors to avoid coming face-to-face with their real selves, seeing reflections as less of a reality to their true appearances than the images they post. Instead of perfect noses and shiny smiles, their faces begin to morph, turning influencers into caricatures that no longer resemble who they used to be.

Noses become crooked as people straighten them, and teeth begin to fall out as hopefuls try to whiten them with a digital brush. Lips crack as humanity paints over them with bright filters, and foreheads wrinkle as apps are used to smooth out natural features.

All the filters Centriclist users spend a fortune on turn them into people they no longer recognize nor are proud of. The need to falsify how they really look on social media has brought out their true inner beauty.

Remi sighs as he leaves the kitchen, wiping his hands on a Ysekes-designed towel. Iris is only twenty-years old. If she continues altering her photos at this rate, she will soon look like the ugly doll hanging over their mantle that haunts them in their sleep every night.

Remi snatches the phone from Iris before she can alter another picture and holds it high above his head, tempted to press "post" but fearful that it will also cause his sister a loss in followers.

Iris turns around with a scowl, her arms crossed over her chest. "Hey! Give that back! I need to keep up my appearances! My followers are already getting suspicious! I'm under deep fire right now. Don't fuck this up for me!"

Remi rolls his eyes, "I've been watching you shrink, extend, and polish your selfies for the last twenty minutes. This is how you end up like the rest of the zombies in this town, hiding in their homes, only to walk outside with scarves over their faces. Do you want to shrivel up and turn into one of them, never being able to show your face in public anymore, all just to impress the Internet? Do you really want to become one of them?"

Iris mocks Remi with her hand, refusing to listen to anything her ignorant brother has to say, and leaps up in attempts to grab her phone. As her twin, Remi is only 20 minutes older than her, yet, he acts like he's 20 years older.

"Just give it to me. I'm not hurting anyone. You just don't get it. You're a guy. You don't need to put as much effort into your pictures as I do!"

Iris is right. Men are held at much lower standards than women when it comes to social media appearances. All men need to do is not fuck up by saying something stupid, and they're almost guaranteed to not lose followers.

Remi switches the phone to his other hand. "Come on, even you know this is ridiculous."

As he speaks, a small red light begins to beep against his temple.

Her bottom lip juts out as Iris crosses her arms over her chest. "You're ridiculous. I have to do this. Do you want me to die? We already lost mom and dad. Do you want me to shatter with them!? Now give me back my phone! I need to make my lips bigger!"

"Not gonna happen, Iris."

Remi walks into the kitchen and places the phone on the cutting board. Iris follows him to the doorway, her complaints a constant whine as he digs through the many drawers.

If Mom was still alive, she would have known how to handle this better. She would have known exactly what to say to Iris instead of doing what I'm about to do.

"I'm doing this for your own good, Iris." He raises a rusty hammer above his head as she begins to scream and plead. "You heard it on the news. You know people who continue altering their selfies will eventually become unrecognizable and grotesque. Do you want that to happen to you?"

"Please, Remi, no. I promise, I won't alter any more of my pictures." Iris jumps forward, trying to swipe the phone, but Remi holds her off with one hand. "I need my phone! You can't do this! You can't take away my phone, or I'll shatter! Don't you understand!?"

"I don't believe in this crap. Everyone says we'll shatter if we don't obey, but I have yet to see that happen. I think we're all just brainwashed into following some dumb rules with consequences that will never come to fruition.

If I let you continue on like this, you'll turn into a shell of yourself. You won't be you anymore. You have become so obsessed with how you look that your personality and reality fade away. Just look at you! You're turning into someone I can't even bare to look at. You look like a dead person walking. You look like the rest of this damn town. I'm not going to let that happen to you, Iris. Enough is enough."

Remi slams the hammer down against the phone, shards of glass and pieces of microchips flying everywhere. Iris cries out, grabbing onto herself to brace her body from shattering into a million pieces like the phone just had.

To her surprise, she's still there. Iris continues to feel around her chest and hips, but every part of her, her arms and legs included, are all still there. Remi grabs the garbage can and sweeps the pieces into it, dropping the trash bin at her feet.

"I told you so. You're fine. These rules, these societies, are all brainwashing you. I don't know how you discovered these obscene filters and apps, but they will not make another appearance in this apartment. Do you understand what I'm saying to you?"

"Yes," Iris spits out as she pulls herself together. "You want me to die. I get it. I'm already ugly. What's the point of living anyway?"

Remi slams his fists down on the counter, his shoulders heaving as he tries to steady his breathing.

"You just don't get it, do you? The point of all this is to be present in the now, not so attached to your Internet appearance that you miss out on the life happening around you every single day. But no, you would rather have your nose stuck in a phone, catering to a bunch of strangers who don't even know you!"

"At least my followers support me!" Iris storms to her room, slamming the door behind her.

"I just saved you from becoming the Wicked Witch of the West!"

WILL THEY EVER LEARN?

The thunderstorm roars, wind blowing against Remi's brown spiked hair. He sits on a rocking chair on his patio, watching through binoculars to seek out those who still look normal amongst hundreds of grotesque-looking crowds. They all look so dead, so out of it, as their noses continue to enlarge, and their asses continue to droop.

What's wrong with this world?

Remi has no clear recollection of the life he had before the apocalypse, but he continues to feel an itch that something is wrong, that this world is not what it seems to be.

He watches as one woman takes a selfie, plays around on her phone for several minutes, and soon after, her face morphs, cheeks dropping low and jowls extending. Her skin becomes baggy, spilling out of her tight club dress, and her heels crack under her newly developed weight. It isn't until her hair begins to fall out and fly away with the wind does she realize what is happening.

Remi hears a shrill scream as the woman drops her phone in attempts to catch her hair. However, it doesn't matter anymore. No one truly cares about their physical appearances anyway. As long as their social images look amazing, that's all that matters.

For those who have really been affected, leaving their homes becomes another common anxiety, much like the worry of one of their followers catching them in real life. Even then, no one would be able to recognize one another.

Surprisingly, it's the same people who alter their images the most who are the ones who become the most mortified of change.

Remi sighs and hangs his binoculars up as the woman continues to scream. He would have to go over and make sure she is okay even though he is certain he would only have the same insane conversation he has every time this happens.

Once, it had been a near-daily occurrence. Now, as most of the town hides in darkened homes, he only sees it once every two or three weeks.

The puddles of rain drench his sandals as he crosses the field in front of his yard and across the street. Behind some large trees, Remi can see bulging eyes watching him, probably too ashamed by their looks to reveal themselves to the public as they continue to post their images in the darkness of the night.

A chill runs down his spine as he presses on, not wanting to think about others lurking around him, out of sight.

"Ma'am?" Remi screams over and over until his voice finally pierces through her screaming.

He comes to a stop beside her and stares at her through the strong winds brushing across his eyes. "Are you okay?"

Her eyes dart to where her phone rests beside her. He resists the urge to kick it farther away.

When will they learn that all their vanity only brings out the ugliness residing within them?

He tries his best to hide the smirk that brushes across his face as these "humans" continue to fall victim to the rules of modern society.

"Ma'am, are you okay?" Remi forces himself to ask again, covering the sarcasm behind his voice and wondering what stupid response would come out of her mouth.

She flattens down the hair that is still on her head and wipes away her tears, her face contorting as she feels how loose the skin has become.

"Do I look okay? How's my lipstick? Is this picture good enough for my Centriclist profile? I really need to gain some new followers."

Tired of her obnoxious ego, Remi looks down at the phone pressed in front of his face. He can easily snatch it away from her and have it against a tree before she knows what is happening.

But what's the point? She, like many others, including Iris, would go out the next day and just buy another phone. It's not like they can survive in this world without one. They just lack the willpower to prevent themselves from being so insecure. There is no doubt about it. Half her head is missing, and all she can focus on is her social media profile.

Yet, he fails to think of anything to say in that moment. So, to break the silence, he takes the phone from her hand and pretends to examine her altered photo.

The woman watches, eyes wide as he breathes in before pitching the evil little piece of technology against the largest tree he can see. That can be considered his good deed for the day for all he cares. Nothing had felt better all day than watching her tears burst forth as the phone is forever shattered into the night.

"Why the fuck did you do that?" She bellows as she dusts off the fallen strands of hair from her shoulders, holding her chin high as particles on her body begins to dissipate fast. "Now I have to go buy another one."

Remi's mouth drops open, shocked that the woman is unaware that she is disappearing before his very eyes.

"Listen, lady, maybe if you weren't so concerned about how you look to the Internet, you wouldn't now resemble a palliative care patient in the cancer ward. Understand?"

He twists on his heel and walks across the field back to his apartment, eager to steer away from the shallow tidal tornado that is humanity.

THE DOWNFALL OF IRIS

Remi cannot believe his eyes when he walks through his front door. There, spread out over their white velvet couch, is Iris, posing for her selfies like she always is.

How did she even get another phone this quickly? Where did she get the money for it? Lord knows I can't make that girl get a job. I've tried. I'm going to wring her neck for this little stunt.

Remi slams the door behind him, throwing his soaked sandals into the corner of the living room.

"And just what exactly do you think you're doing?"

Iris jumps, the phone nearly flying out of her hand as she snaps another picture of herself. Remi stares, his eyes wide, as the filters she had recently applied to her pictures finally catch up to her.

Her eyes become too large for her head, a swampy green instead of the beautiful emerald they had once been. Her hair had lost its curl, and her skin tone becomes sickly.

Any fat in her face is leeched away as she becomes sunken and hollow while the fat on her hips become engorged. He can see the dips in her temples where she had once been, now covered in the remnants of a corpse. The top half of her body looks like a malnourished child, halfway to her grave, while her lower half resembles that of a whale.

"What happened?" Her words are slow as if her tongue had become too heavy for her mouth.

Remi watches as the energy for life drains from her, all the while, her follower counts gradually increase.

Iris lifts one gnarled hand, looking at the way the joints now curve and bend. Her eyes are filled with tears as she examines the unnatural way her fingers now twist from her swollen hands. Her whole body is contorted and wrong.

This isn't who she is supposed to be. This isn't who she is!

Remi stares at the person in front of him, his twin sister, unrecognizable, the one woman in the world he is supposed to protect from all evil.

Instead, he had failed her. She wasted away to a creature that no longer resembles her true self, all just to impress strangers and become an Internet celebrity.

Maybe he should have told her how beautiful she was, told her how funny, smart, and bright. Maybe if he had tried just a little bit harder to make her understand that there was more to life than the way she looked then, maybe, she would still be the sister he remembers.

Now, she looks like one of the zombies crawling around beneath the bleachers at work, or those who only appear in the middle of the night seeking attention.

"What did I do?" Her sobs pour hard and fast, her whole body shaking as she curls in on herself in the corner of the couch. "What have I done? I'm ugly now. I've always been ugly."

Remi takes a seat beside her, pulling her into a tight embrace.

"It's going to be okay, Iris. You're still an amazing young woman. How you look doesn't matter. I promise. You are still amazing, smart, and funny. Way smarter than I am. We'll get through this, I promise."

She sobs harder, her grotesque hands forming fists in his shirt.

"I just wanted to be beautiful. I wanted to know that I was beautiful. You wouldn't understand at all. You've never cared about trying. You can look like yourself as much as you want with no makeup or filters, and people would still love you."

Remi gently smooths his hand over her thinning and greasy hair, trying not to wince at the texture against his palm.

"It's not all it's cracked up to be, Iris. It's just that I don't care anymore. I know exactly what I look like and hate every minute of it. You just need to push it aside and move on. There's less pressure to be the person you actually are."

Iris untangles herself and stands up, moving slower than a sloth. "You don't get it. I'm going to bed."

LOST CAUSE OF HUMANITY

Sassas Foothills is his last attempt to cheer Iris up, a beautiful mountain range where all the social media aspirants flock to if they want to resemble someone worth resembling.

She had spent all day for the past week in her room, only emerging to take her selfies on the white sofa. She refused to speak or go near the doorway of the apartment.

His sister has become a hollow shell of a person, like the majority of those in this town. She remains hidden behind everything, only fully emerging at night when the dark makes it too difficult to properly see her prominent features.

Remi sits on the edge of a cliff, his feet dangling above the city, and his arms slung back to keep him from toppling over. For a moment, he had a grim thought of one of the lurkers pushing him over the edge just so they can take an epic picture for the 'list.

Yes, this is a thing. People are willing to go through any lengths to become the best. He has grown used to seeing what looks like slightly hydrated shrunken heads, but it is all still unsettling.

His stomach turns as he twists to watch Iris take images of her feet dangling over the ledge behind him, her face covered with a silk scarf, now that she has become too horrific to look at. The hump on her back is prominent as she leans forward to take that perfect aerial shot.

Luckily, everyone there is too focused on chasing after their own perfect posts to pay attention to the oddly-shaped woman beside them, not like many of them aren't also oddly-shaped.

Remi looks over by the nearby canyons and sees a man taking his own selfie, an instant beer belly sprouting from his defined abs.

People will never learn. Remi thinks as he turns to look over the cliff once more.

Maybe, one day, things will be different, and whatever this monstrosity is will go away. But what would that solve anyway? Everyone is already too far gone. It's not like there's a magic potion to reverse all this.

"Mind if I take a seat?" A melodic voice that brightens his dreams and perishes his nightmares pours from over his shoulder.

He twists to see the most beautiful woman he has ever laid eyes on standing behind him in a lace bikini. What she is doing in a bikini in the middle of the mountains is beyond his knowledge, but he doesn't care. She is magnificent.

"Sure," he says. "I haven't seen you around this area before. Are you new?" Remi asks as he remains stricken with love over her beauty.

"I'm new in town, just moved from a few counties over. It was getting kind of lame there. I needed a change. I'm Kat, short for Katria."

The woman smiles, her arm brushing up against his leg, sending chills down his spine. "Can you believe how many people are obsessed with changing their images? The pictures they end up posting resemble nothing like the pictures they're taking now. That guy over there can have the Eiffel Tower behind him in just two seconds. It's so crazy!"

His eyes broaden as he falls more in love.

"Finally, a woman with some sense! I'm Remi. You know, I've heard and said all the things they say about the people who ruin themselves with taking selfies and altering images. I've made fun of their depression, or their hiding in the shadows and avoiding the public eye. I've focused on the fact that it is their fault, and not the fact that they don't deserve to be treated like they aren't people anymore.

Now, over half our population is completely different from the people they were born as, faces unrecognizable and difficult to look at. Yet, what do we do? We continue to judge ourselves and others for the way we look.

Even my own sister has to live with that. She has to deal with the staring and pointing of fingers. She's going to hear all the jokes made at her expense. She's only twenty, and this is going to ruin her for life. She will grow up thinking the worst because that is what everybody is going to tell her. They won't act like they like her because she looks different. What am I supposed to do?"

Katria reaches over and takes his hand, "What you do now, is you love her. Don't make her feel any different. She's going to have bad days. You're going to want to say or do hurtful things, so is she. She has to adjust to life looking like a completely different person now. You've never had to do that. Make her know her feelings are valid, and that she is safe with you."

Remi runs his thumb over the back of her hand, "You sound like you're speaking from experience."

Katria smiles. "I learned pretty fast that I had been wrong about a lot of things. Oddly, it took a couple selfies to see what really matters in life, years of realizing that I don't need constant validation to be okay with myself."

From behind a rock, one of the strange-looking shrunken heads stare at him, a gap-filled smile spreading. He doesn't know who this person is or why she is watching from the shadows.

Suddenly, Katria leans over and passionately kisses his lips, sending him into another dimension as ecstasy fills his body, and he instantly forgets why he was so angry. It is as if something has possessed his body with passion.

He raises his hands to her face and strokes her hair, laying her down onto the patch of grass beside them, gliding his lips across the nape of her neck.

As he does so, he hears a soft whisper, "It's time to forget."

Unsure of what's going on, Remi suddenly feels different, a strange sensation rushing over his body as a drop of blood leaks from his right eye before he wipes it away with the back of his hand.

"Remi, I think I want to leave now," Iris runs over to Remi and gestures him.

However, Remi does not recognize the strange woman in front of him, the same strange woman who was lurking from the shadows moments before. This ugly creature pulling on his arm is enough to make him vomit over her grotesqueness.

"Ew, what the hell are you?! Get away from me, you hag!" Remi pulls his arm away from the creature.

Her face skeletal, her legs enlarged like an elephant, and with features like a hyena, Iris tries to remind Remi who she is.

"Remi, it's me, Iris. Your sister. Come on, stop messing around. I need to leave."

Still disgusted by the creature in front of him, Remi pushes Iris over a large boulder.

"Get away from me, you repulsive THING. Don't ever come near me again! Come on, Kat, let's get out of here."

As Remi and Katria walk back to his apartment, the townspeople become stranger and stranger. One by one, people who used to be friends and acquaintances no longer recognize each other.

Their social media feeds remain the same, with the same glamourous pictures they have always posted, but the people behind the cameras look completely different.

"Excuse me, have you seen Sketch?" A man dressed in a business suit asks another man dressed in athleisure wear.

"What are you talking about, man? It's me, Sketch!"

"Nah, you're messing with me. Excuse me, miss, have you seen Sketch?"

The man in the suit walks toward a woman in question, leaving Sketch behind to question how his best friend has forgotten about him as he pulls his beanie over his face in shame.

"Come on, we need to hurry. Iris is home all alone, and she is not well right now. I need to see if she's okay." Remi rushes.

Not remembering the incident that had just transpired, Remi walks inside the apartment and shouts out to Iris. No response. He searches all the rooms, but still, no one is to be found.

"That's weird. She should be here. 3pm is when she always takes her selfies on the couch. Iris! Iris!!"

No response.

"I'm sure she'll show up eventually. She's probably just hanging out with some friends. You know how these Centriclist influencers are," Katria reassures Remi as she sits him on the velvet sofa and rubs his shoulders. "You're just stressed. It's all going to be okay, I promise."

Katria then leans over Remi's right shoulder and kisses him passionately once again, sending chills up and down his body. Remi becomes lost in a daze as his mind floats from the love he experiences, failing to think of anything else but making sweet love to Katria.

He flips her over onto her back and nibbles on her neck, slowly making his way down to her breasts before undressing her. He glides his hands up and down her thighs, pressing his naked body up and in against her, thrusting his hips in and out, and kissing her breasts, until he feels a sharp pain in his pelvis.

Stunned, he pulls back and sees a black liquid beginning to leak out of Katria's pelvis, with her eyes soon to follow.

"I've been waiting for you, Remi. You're a tough one to find, but I finally have you in my grips." Katria whispers eerily, closing in on Remi.

"Who...who are you?! What are you?" Remi stutters as he quickly backs away from the being before him.

"Don't you remember me? We were part of an experiment together, you, me, Iris, and a few others who have long been destroyed by a group known as 'Witness'.

We were all survivors of the deadly virus that overtook the nation, destroying everyone except for a few, and created a world of fakes in the process. We were supposed to work together.

Witness wanted to re-create the apocalyptic moment and generate a new virus that would turn us humans into monsters whenever we alter an image.

We made a pact to work together. We were supposed to help each other get out of that hellhole. But, instead, you and your damn sister threw the rest of us under the bus, sending us straight into the arms of the enemies by tricking us to turn ourselves in while you two made a run for it.

They tested gravely on the rest of us, injecting chemical after chemical into our bodies with pain that was unbearable. After several trials and endless torture, I became the only one left. My DNA had bound to the virus, and I began to respond to the results they wanted.

However, they failed to test their virus completely, and it began to malfunction. Those infected by this new virus would go through endless stages of contorted transformations before finally shattering into pieces themselves, despite not having any loss in followers. That was only a ploy.

People have become so sickening and obsessed with the perfect photos that they forget that it's their very obsession that destroys them. Poor Iris, probably dead now, all that vain, and nothing to show for it. I know you're probably thinking, why haven't I changed?

Well, I did. There was a time when I was equally obsessed with filters. My body transformed to creatures I cannot even imagine. I became a horrific monster, strolling the Earth like a mindless zombie. But then they saved me.

They came along. Gave me hope, a serum to reverse this virus if I can just get them their prize. You. For some odd reason, mind-blowing to everyone, you cannot be tempted by popularity and fame, yet, you remain alive.

Why? We need to find out what makes you so special, what makes you not turn," Katria finishes.

"Look, I don't know who the fuck you are, but you're not taking me anywhere!" Remi exclaims in fear as crimson blood drips from the corners of his eyes once more. "Stay away from me!"

"But we made love, Remi. You can trust me. You can trust that I know what's best for you. We connected." Kat closes in.

"Get away from me, you freak!" Remi throws a lamp at Katria as he bolts out the door, most of the town desolate as people have turned to hiding inside their homes to avoid showing their monstrosities to the world.

The world has become different now, a world no one can recognize. Remi continues running toward nowhere until his legs finally give out.

He finds himself keeled over a lake, his reflection shining back at him as he surprisingly sees Iris, the real Iris, not the freak he had been living with, standing next to him.

Remi looks up and faces a mysterious being who resembles his alter ego.

"Iris," he whispers, as his face cracks and reveals a series of microchips and barbed wires beneath it.

Death by Vanity
Be Careful What You Change

Death by Vanity
Be Careful What You Change